Eleanor was stunned to see the Comte de Beauvais standing before her. *"Ma chere,"* he said, raising her hand to his lips. "Why did you not wait for me in Dover?"

Anger sparkled in Eleanor's eyes. "Monsieur le Comte, I have no idea what you are talking about. I came to Brussels with Lydia Milford and arrived to discover a ridiculous rumor that I had made plans to run away with you." Eleanor forced herself to laugh. "Monsieur, the notion that I would run away with you is absurd."

But the comte refused to retreat. "You are angry with me. You feel I failed you by arriving too late. Please, please, believe me," Beauvais declared, still holding onto her hand. "My love for you is as strong as ever."

Eleanor felt his touch, heard his words, and grew flushed. But could she trust this man who had almost ruined her once? And even more important, could she trust herself . . . ?

MISS REDMOND'S FOLLY

APRIL KIHLSTROM

A SIGNET BOOK

NEW AMERICAN LIBRARY

SIGNET TRADEMARK REG. U.S.PAT. OFF. AND FOREIGN COUNTRIES
REGISTERED TRADEMARK—MARCA REGISTRADA
HECHO EN CHICAGO, U.S.A.

SIGNET, SIGNET CLASSIC, MENTOR, ONYX, PLUME, MERIDIAN and
NAL BOOKS ARE PUBLISHED BY NAL PENGUIN INC.,
1633 BROADWAY, NEW YORK, NEW YORK 10019

First Printing, June, 1988

1 2 3 4 5 6 7 8 9

PRINTED IN THE UNITED STATES OF AMERICA

1

Eleanor Redmond was one of the most delightful of the new crop of young ladies to appear for the London Season in the spring of 1815. That was the considered opinion of the majority of gentlemen who took great interest in such things. Miss Redmond was petite, blond, with large blue eyes, a perfectly proportioned figure, and possessed of a ready smile. Unfortunately, none of the many gentlemen who fell victim to Miss Redmond's charms seemed capable of causing her to fall victim to theirs. Wagers ran high as to whether anyone would ever capture Miss Redmond's heart if, in fact, she had one. It was perhaps inevitable that someone would take up the gauntlet in earnest.

Miss Redmond, the object of all this attention was, one late spring afternoon, looking through her wardrobe with her maid. She was tired, having had of late, like any girl in her first Season, far less sleep than she needed. As a result, she was not her usual cheerful self. "No, no, Anna," Miss Redmond said, feeling very close to tears. "The

Comte de Beauvais has seen me in every one of those! I simply must have my new gowns. Hasn't Mademoiselle Suzette delivered any of them yet?"

"No, Miss Redmond," Anna replied with well-practiced patience. "And if you ask me, you are altogether too concerned with what this Frenchy will think."

Eleanor's younger sister, Amanda, who had been watching from a window seat with great interest, immediately said, "Well she didn't ask you, Anna. And I think you should go to Mademoiselle Suzette's establishment and get Nora's new dresses right now. Tell her that Nora simply must have them today."

Anna directed a quelling look at the girl. Quietly she said, "No, Miss Amanda, I won't. It wouldn't do a ha'penny's worth of good anyway. Mademoiselle Suzette said they would be ready Thursday, and Thursday they will be. Not a day sooner."

"But I tell you I want them today!" Eleanor cried.

"And I tell you there is nothing to be done about it," Anna replied calmly.

"You shall go and get her dresses, Anna, or we won't have you as our maid anymore," Amanda threatened, a steely glint in her eye.

Tranquilly Anna replied, "You both know very well my orders come from your mother, and Lady Redmond has no desire to see me go." She paused and softened her voice as she looked at Eleanor's distressed face. "There, there, pet, you're feeling all tired out with all this partying and dancing and such, I don't doubt. No, nor is it easy fancying yourself in love, with all the ups and downs that go with *that*, I'll warrant. It's no wonder you're

6

feeling out of sorts," she said kindly. "But I've no doubt the dresses will be ready tomorrow and you shall dazzle your fine beau then. For today you must be patient."

Amanda started to protest again and Eleanor moved to intervene. With a tiny sigh she said, "Very well, Anna. Please take the green dress and press it. I shall have to wear that tonight."

"Very good, Miss Redmond," Anna replied serenely as she took up the required gown and left.

Meanwhile Amanda noted the admonitory look in her sister's eyes and hastily set about to distract her. "Do you think you will see him tonight?" she asked eagerly as she moved to sit on the edge of the bed and clasp the post.

"Of course Jean-Pierre will be there," Eleanor replied at once. "He said so." She paused and added ruefully, "Which has put me in a terrible temper, I fear, and all because I've nothing new to wear. Bother Mademoiselle Suzette, anyway! He's seen every dress I have at least once already."

"Perhaps Jean-Pierre won't mind," Amanda answered hopefully. "If I were in love with someone, I shouldn't care what they wore."

Eleanor shrugged unhappily. "But he does care. He always notices what I wear and tells me if he thinks my dress has begun to seem shabby or lacks the latest furbclows or doesn't become me. Sometimes I think I shall never satisfy him."

"Perhaps it would be best if he did stop liking you," Amanda replied, with the wisdom of her thirteen years. "You know Mama and Papa don't like him, Nora. Not in the least."

"Then they are absolutely heartless, and so are you to agree with them," Eleanor retorted, beginning to cry. "They've never been fair to Jean-Pierre. They just don't understand how we feel."

"Well, I do," Amanda declared loyally.

"Do you?" Eleanor asked hopefully. Then her shoulders sagged as she added, "In any event, what does that matter? You can't help me." Before Amanda could answer Eleanor sat on the bed beside her sister and said eagerly, "But you do like Jean-Pierre, don't you? You do think he's wonderfully handsome? And so generous?"

A trifle doubtfully Amanda stared at her hands. "Perhaps too generous, sometimes. You know what Mama said when she saw that bracelet he wanted to give you." Then, noting the thunderous look darkening her sister's face, Amanda hastened to add, "But he is handsome. Quite the most handsome gentleman I've ever seen. When I'm eighteen, I should like to fall in love with someone like that. Tall but not too tall. Hair dark and not an insipid brown. With an air of mystery and an accent that makes one quite shiver with delight."

The two girls shivered together and then fell to discussing how Eleanor might wear her hair to dazzle him.

The gentleman in question, the Comte de Beauvais, was equally preoccupied with the question of Miss Redmond. At the same moment that she was talking with Amanda in her room, he was surrounded by acquaintances and listening as their talk swirled about the topic of his success with that young lady. For the past three weeks he had been the favored suitor, and formal wagers had been recorded at a number of gaming halls in London as to whether he would succeed in marrying her.

Only a select few, however, knew about the other wager, the one the count had made himself.

Beauvais had no intention of marrying Miss Redmond. His tastes did not run in that direction nor, in any event, did he believe that her parents would ever accept an offer from him for her hand. But he thought he saw a way to line his pockets and at the same time enjoy a joke at her expense. It might well be said that he was looking forward to the evening with even greater anticipation than Miss Redmond herself.

Meanwhile, Lady Redmond was also preoccupied with thoughts of her eldest daughter's future, for that was why, after all, they were in London. It had certainly not been Eleanor's idea. She had not asked her parents to rent an extremely expensive house in the best part of town. Eleanor would have been content to stay closer to home and marry someone like Sir Elbert's son. But Lady Redmond had been more ambitious for her eldest daughter, and that was the rub. Lady Redmond had not brought Eleanor to London out of concern that she might later regret not having had the chance to look about her at the young men there; she had been brought to London to make a more advantageous match than to a mere baronet's son. Only Eleanor steadfastly refused to accept any of the suitors her mother had brought to her attention. Instead, she insisted upon befriending the most appalling fellows. And that had led to several rows between mother and daughter.

As she told her bosom bow, Lady Denville, "Of course I could not allow Nora to throw herself away on a country nobody, and I will not allow her to do the same or worse here in London either."

"But has she been sincerely attached to any of the young men?" Lady Denville asked.

"I think not, but what if she were?" Lady Redmond replied less than tranquilly. "I would still not agree to have a mere baronet's son as a son-in-law, not when Nora can hope to look much higher. Nor a penniless refugee. How would it look if I settled for such a poor match for my eldest daughter? That is not why I brought Nora to London or told Lord Redmond his relatives must procure us vouchers for Almack's. I knew they would hardly like to have us denied admission there. And Nora may still make a match we can be proud of."

Given these views, it is no surprise that Lady Redmond paid great attention to her eldest daughter's appearance as well as behavior. Shortly before they were due to leave for Almack's, on the same night Eleanor had had her conversation with Amanda, Lady Remond appeared in Eleanor's room to see that her toilette was completed properly and that the girl had not overlooked anything. Pearls at her ears and throat were the right touch, Lady Redmond agreed, though privately she thought it a pity Nora was too young to wear emeralds. Still, her gown of green satin and lace, matching slippers, and long gloves suited Nora's delicate features. Her hair was done up in curls atop her head and she carried a painted fan procured for her by her father.

"But this one sent me by Jean-Pierre is much prettier," Eleanor said hesitantly, holding out another fan.

Lady Redmond's lips tightened in disapproval as she replied, "Mere trumpery! You will carry the one your father gave you. I will not have you putting off other suitors, as you shall if you appear to single out the Comte de Beauvais for

10

approval. You are not to waltz with him at all. Though should the Viscount Halliwell ask you, that is an entirely different matter and you have my permission to stand up with him. He has a most excellent estate and a handsome income from his father's trusts."

"I will not stand up with Halliwell," Eleanor replied with dignity. "I shall dance with Jean-Pierre instead and you cannot stop me."

"No?" Lady Redmond asked, her voice dangerously quiet.

For a long moment they stood with eyes locked together. Then, her own voice quiet, Eleanor said, with a sigh, "Very well, I promise I shall not dance with Jean-Pierre. But you have no objection, I trust, if I talk with him?"

"Certainly not," Lady Redmond agreed. "It would be remarked upon if you were to cut the Comte de Beauvais completely, and I should find that quite disagreeable. As when you refused to speak with the Marquess of Alnwick. Really, child, that was too bad of you. You might have at least made a push to be polite to him."

Eleanor wrinkled her nose. "Ugh," she said. "He is the most disagreeable man I have ever met. I didn't wish to be polite to him. Besides, he just laughed."

"True," Lady Redmond agreed. "And that could only help you. Nevertheless, I should not like you to get a reputation for being fickle rather than merely particular. But you know well enough what I mean, and I shan't worry you anymore over it. Come along, Nora, your papa will have the carriage waiting by now." She paused then added dryly, "You will also not address the Comte de Beauvais as Jean-Pierre."

"Yes, Mama," Eleanor said soberly. Then, with a sparkle in her eye, she said defiantly, "Shouldn't we be going, Mama? After all, we wouldn't want to be late."

"Don't be impertinent, child," Lady Redmond retorted sharply as she stood in the doorway to her daughter's room. "I am only thinking of you. The earlier we arrive, the more gentlemen who will have the opportunity to dance with you. Though by now I suppose it is very unlikely we will see any gentlemen you have not already met. A pity the Season is so far advanced. I had hoped by now that you would have managed to bring *someone* up to scratch that you—and we—found acceptable."

"Sir Elbert's son would have come up to scratch," Eleanor answered quietly.

Lady Redmond gave her daughter a speaking look. "Don't mention that boy's name to me, Nora. I said someone acceptable. Now, come along or we shall be late."

2

Aᴠᴛᴇʀ Lᴏʀᴅ Rᴇᴅᴍᴏɴᴅ'ꜱ relatives had procured the necessary vouchers for Almack's, Eleanor had not been allowed to miss even one of the Wednesday-evening subscription balls. This particular evening they were among the first families to arrive and exchange a few polite words with the patronesses.

Jean-Pierre, the Comte de Beauvais, on the other hand, arrived shortly before the doors were closed at eleven o'clock when Lady Redmond was engaged in conversation with a friend so that he was able to seek out Eleanor unobserved by her mama. He sauntered about the room casually greeting friends and flattering the ladies until he had positioned himself where Miss Redmond's current partner would be likely to end up when the music stopped. Then it was a simple matter of stepping forward and claiming the next dance.

Miss Redmond blushed charmingly and looked down at the floor as she replied in a soft voice, "I should like to, monsieur, but I have promised my mama I will not dance with you tonight."

13

She swiftly looked up at him to see if he had taken offense, but the comte was all kindness as he replied, "That is no problem, little one. We shall go and have a glass of punch together, or lemonade. There can be nothing objectionable in something so harmless as that, surely?"

Still blushing, Eleanor shook her head. "I cannot see how anyone could object," she agreed.

As they were speaking, the Viscount Halliwell came up to the pair and with a sharp look at Beauvais said peremptorily, "My dance, I believe, Miss Redmond."

Impulsively, with more emotion than wisdom, Eleanor hastily replied, "I am very sorry, Lord Halliwell, but you see that I am otherwise engaged. Perhaps another time."

Halliwell's eyes sparkled with anger but he was too much the gentleman to do other than bow and withdraw.

Eleanor placed a hand on the count's arm and said, "Shall we find a quiet place to talk?"

Beauvais laughed softly as he led her toward the other room. "Was that wise, *ma petite*? Or kind? You will not forever be a reigning beauty, you know, and a man might take offense. It was, I suppose, his dance?" he added gently.

Eleanor blushed but replied impatiently, "I don't care. I would much rather be with you. Do you see any reason why I shouldn't?"

Again Beauvais laughed softly. "No, but then, *ma chère*, I should dislike to see you dance or speak with anyone save myself, so I can scarcely be fair about the matter, can I?"

Abruptly Eleanor halted and clutched his arm tighter as she said, "Oh, Jean-Pierre, I wish we were done with this nonsense. I cannot bear Mama telling me I am not to encourage you or dance with you or even allow you to call upon me at home. What are we to do? I cannot bear it, I tell you! Sometimes I almost wish we could run away together, be married secretly, and to the devil with everyone else in the world!"

Swiftly Beauvais looked around him, but there was no one close enough to overhear their conversation, though one or two ladies were casting speculative glances in their direction. He spoke as quickly as he could, "Do you mean that, *ma chère*? Of course you do, and I am foolish to doubt you. Oh, I wish the same thing sometimes, but I know far too well that it would not be fair of me to ask you to do it. To run away with me and ruin yourself."

"Ask me," Eleanor insisted huskily.

Again Beauvais looked around before he went on, "Very well. If you have the courage, *ma petite*, and the love for me, meet me on the packet going to Ostend from Dover the day after tomorrow. You will have to leave tomorrow, and alone, for I am certain your parents are having me watched and if they see us together they will stop us for certain. You go on ahead and I shall join you on board the ship. The *Golden Mermaid*. I will have a friend of mine pay the passage for you. You are not to worry about a thing." He paused and looked downcast as he added, "Of course, if your courage or your love is not strong enough, *ma chère*, I shall understand and go away so that you need never be troubled by me again."

All Eleanor's doubts were swept away with the need to convince Jean-Pierre that she did love him and did possess courage. "I shall be there," she said fiercely. "I swear I shall not fail you."

Beauvais lifted her hand to kiss it but was stopped before he could do so by Lady Redmond's stern voice saying loudly, "Ah, there you are, Eleanor. Beauvais, how kind of you to take her in charge, but as you see, I am here now and can take charge of her myself. Good day, monsieur."

Beauvais merely bowed and relinquished the girl into her mother's care. He was markedly cheerful as he then strolled away, causing Lady Redmond's eyes to narrow in suspicion. "Eleanor," she asked ominously, "what are the two of you up to now? Why does the comte look so pleased with himself?"

Miss Redmond avoided her mother's eyes. But Lady Redmond did not wait for an answer. Instead, her eyes continued to follow the count as he found another young lady to talk to, and after observing his animated features while he was flattering the chit, she was satisfied. "Good. He is beginning to show an interest in someone other than you. Now, come along and dance. Several young men are looking for you, Nora."

Meekly the girl did as she was bid, thankful that her mother was so easily satisfied. As she danced, however, during the next few hours Eleanor's thoughts were occupied with schemes of how to escape from the house and make her way to Dover. She had never traveled on her own before, but in theory it should not be that difficult, she supposed. Fortunately it was not two days since that Papa had given her pin money, and that sum still rested in her reticule at home. Surely it would be enough to take her to Dover, and once Jean-Pierre joined her aboard the packet, he would take care of all their needs.

For a brief moment the thought did occur to

Eleanor that she ought to plan for the possibility that Jean-Pierre might be unavoidably delayed in joining her, but a quick mental calculation assured her that the sum in her reticule would be sufficient for a week or more even if Jean-Pierre should be delayed that long. Which was, of course, unthinkable.

So it was in excellent if a trifle preoccupied spirits that Eleanor spent the rest of the evening and journey home with her parents. Lord and Lady Redmond could not help but congratulate their daughter on her ladylike behavior. Aside from the encounter with Halliwell, which neither had seen, Eleanor had been extremely polite to the young gentlemen who formed her court. She had even agreed prettily—if a trifle absentmindedly—to the various suggestions that had been put forward to entertain her over the next several days.

Meanwhile, the Comte de Beauvais had his own arrangements to make. He waited until after the Redmond party had left Almack's and then he left to seek out certain close friends who had chosen to spend the evening playing cards instead. He found them at a private house given over to card and gaming parties and known for its success in relieving green country-bred gentlemen of their funds. The count's friends, however, did not fall into that category and in fact had enjoyed a moderate success at the tables.

Beauvais joined them and it was almost dawn when the men left the house. They were beyond feeling any pain, for the couple who ran the gaming house were generous with their wine. No one, however, could have described the men as castaway. Indeed, Beauvais was quite capable of laying out his plan for his friends, so that by the time the men parted company at the street that held their respective lodgings, all was arranged. And with a final laugh they all sought their beds.

In another part of London Lydia Milford was making her arrangements to travel across the channel to join her husband, Colonel Jason Milford, who was with Wellington's army in Europe. He had assured her that it would be safe for her to come to Brussels, though he warned her he could not say how much time they would have together. Lydia was determined to go. And just as determined to take her brother with her. "After all, it is not as though you have anything important to do here in London," she told him crossly when he objected.

"Yes, but I don't wish to go," he retorted good-naturedly. "Besides, I thought Milford's brother was escorting you."

Lydia flung herself into a chair petulantly as she said, "Yes, well, his wife has chosen this, of all times, to go into labor and have her baby. There should have been plenty of time for him to escort me there and then come back before the baby was born. Now it's hopeless and I won't delay my trip," she added, forestalling her brother's next suggestion.

"Oh, Freddy, please come with me," Lydia said, trying a different tack. "Jason has told me I am absolutely not to travel alone, and if I do, he shall send me straight back home again. And it's been too long since I saw him. I know you don't want to go, but I swear you won't have to stay in Brussels, just take me that far. Who knows, perhaps you'll meet some fascinating young lady there and lose your heart at last."

At her brother's snort of disbelief Lydia went on, "It would do you good, you know. As Papa's heir it's about time you settled down and produced a son of your own. Otherwise, who is to inherit if something happens to you? Cousin Wilfred? No, thank you. I should rather see the estates run into the ground. Oh, please come, Freddy, you know I'd rather have you than anyone else anyway."

In the end, Frederick Leverton was not proof against his sister's entreaties. They had always been the best of friends, and he found it hard to deny Lydia's request. Particularly when he knew it meant she would otherwise be unable to go. And it had been two months since she had seen her husband. Colonel Milford had been on leave when Napoleon escaped Elba. Then, since he was a member of Wellington's staff, Jason had hastened back to the Continent, where he was at once put to work acting as courier and, Leverton suspected, spy for the Duke of Wellington. Now, finally, Colonel Milford had been assigned to duty in Brussels. So, in the end, Frederick Leverton found himself promising, when it was already close to dawn that morning, that he would be ready to travel by early afternoon to Brussels.

"But will we have trouble purchasing passage on such short notice?" Frederick asked.

Lydia shook her head. "We shan't need to. Jason's brother did not precisely cancel our tickets. He said he was sure I would be able to persuade you to go."

"You mean he knew you'd succeed in twisting me about your little finger," Frederick retorted wrathfully.

He was, however, grinning and took his leave a few minutes later, whistling as he went. And Lydia Milford sought her own bed with a happy smile upon her face. Within the week she could hope to see her husband again.

3

Much to everyone's surprise, Eleanor Redmond came downstairs early the next morning instead of breakfasting in bed, as was her habit. She then announced that she was going for a drive with Mr. Percy Braden as soon as he should arrive. While they were still absorbing that astonishing pronouncement, Eleanor added that her parents could handle any other suitors who might come to call.

If the truth be told, Eleanor had accepted Braden's invitation to go for that morning drive rather absentmindedly. And when she realized what she had done, she shrugged and assumed she would find some excuse to put him off. But that was only at first. Eleanor had letters to write, to Amanda and to her parents, letters she meant to post from Dover just before she boarded the packet for Ostend. Then she tried to pack her things, at which point she discovered that she had no trunks or boxes or anything of the sort in her room; they were all stored elsewhere in the house and she could not find them on her own nor ask a

servant to bring them without risking someone
telling her parents. The second realization that
came to her was that there was no way she could
walk out of the house carrying trunks or boxes
without the same thing happening. That was the
trouble with being surrounded with servants.

Even if she could have gotten her clothes out of
the house, it had occurred to Eleanor that she
could not ask for the family carriage to take her to
the nearest traveling coach inn, nor did she know
how to summon a hack. The only reason she even
knew about mail coaches was because her various
governesses had always traveled that way to and
from the Redmond home.

Percy Braden appeared to offer a much-needed
solution to the dilemma. He was amiable but not
overly bright. He was quiet also and inclined to do
anything he thought would please, which suited
Eleanor perfectly. And when her parents
inevitably did begin to wonder at her absence,
they would start with a visit to Mr. Braden, who
would be able to tell them very little. Eleanor
Redmond meant to be very clever and very
prudent about her escape so that Jean-Pierre
would be proud of her.

In the end, Eleanor settled for taking her largest
reticule and putting a few necessities inside. If
Mademoiselle Suzette had her newest gowns
ready as promised, Eleanor could take them with
her. Otherwise . . . Well, Jean-Pierre would
provide for her, and surely the clothes he would
buy her on the Continent would be more becoming
anyway.

Thus Eleanor was in excellent spirits when
Percy Braden arrived precisely on time. He bowed
to Eleanor and her mother, flushed with pleasure

as Miss Redmond smiled at him, helped her on with her pelisse, then hastened to follow her out the door and handed her into his curricle before she could change her mind.

As they pulled away from the curb, Eleanor nodded to herself with satisfaction. She was all smiles as he stammered politely, "Wh-where would you like to go, Miss Redmond? A drive about the park, perhaps."

"I should love that," Eleanor said, placing a hand gently on his arm. "Isn't it a glorious day?"

"Y-yes, it is," he replied nervously. "Wouldn't have come 'round to take you for a drive if it wasn't."

Prettily Eleanor pouted. "Do you mean you would have deserted me if it had rained?"

Braden colored. Hastily he said, " 'Course not. Would have come to call, just not taken you for a drive."

"Are you glad you did come to take me for a drive?" Eleanor persisted.

Braden nodded vigorously. "Farnham and Thornley will be surprised. Said they didn't believe you'd really go with me. Said you wouldn't think I was rich enough or handsome enough or daring enough to go out with."

With a frown Eleanor flushed. "Am I really considered as heartless as that?" she asked.

Earnestly Braden replied as he neatly drove his team between the gates of the park, "I don't think so. Told 'em you weren't, in fact. Though I only asked you because Ozzie dared me to. Didn't think you'd really accept. Everyone knows it's that Frenchy you like."

Eleanor's hands clasped each other tightly in her lap and she swallowed hard, forcing herself to laugh as she said brightly, "Indeed? And are you sorry I accepted?"

Braden turned to look at Miss Redmond, and there was a touch of exasperation in his voice as he said, "Now, if that isn't the most henwitted question anyone has ever asked me! How could I be sorry that you are riding in my carriage? I'll have everyone envying me before nightfall."

In spite of herself Eleanor laughed. Her eyes twinkled as she said, "I see. So I am to add to your credit, am I? What a lowering reflection, for here I was thinking that it was my personal charms that attracted you."

"They do." He nodded briefly. "But I'm not such a fool that I don't know you're above m' touch." Then, a trifle aggrieved, he added, "You'll notice I didn't ask you why you agreed to go for a drive with me."

Eleanor had been prepared for that. "Why, I've heard that you tell the most marvelous stories. Won't you tell me one?"

Since that was in fact true, Braden did as he was bid, and the next three-quarters of an hour passed quickly. Eleanor resolutely ignored whatever looks of astonishment were cast in their direction. After that, Eleanor persuaded Braden to drive her to Mademoiselle Suzette's shop near Leicester Square. He was a trifle doubtful, but did as he was bid. When they reached the place he said, "Shall I come in with you?"

Eleanor forced herself to laugh lightly. "No, no, I know how gentlemen detest such establishments. My mama is to meet me here within the hour and I shall wait for her. You have been very kind, but I assure you I shall be fine on my own and you may go home now. Thank you for a most pleasant morning drive. Will you take me for another drive in a week or so?"

Percy Braden was still doubtful, but he was not proof against those upturned eyes, framed by the most delightful lashes. Nor to that unexpected invitation. In the end, feeling a trifle dazed, Braden took his leave of Miss Redmond, waiting only to see that she really did enter Mademoiselle Suzette's establishment.

As she heard the carriage pull away behind her, Eleanor let out a sigh of relief. Then she straightened her shoulders, not at all sure that Mademoiselle Suzette would be as simple a proposition as Mr. Braden had been.

She need not have worried. At the sight of Miss Redmond, Mademoiselle Suzette repressed a sigh of her own and came forward with a smile. It had already been a long, difficult morning for her and she hoped Miss Redmond did not represent one more problem. "*Allô*, my dear Miss Redmond. May I help you? Where is your mama?"

Eleanor smiled in return. With a confidence she did not truly feel she said, "I came to see if my gowns were ready. You *did* promise them for today, and I was tired of waiting. And I was afraid that the messenger might take them to the wrong house or something."

With great effort Mademoiselle Suzette forced herself to answer calmly. "That has never happened, Miss Redmond, and from my establishment it never will. But, yes, the dresses are ready, and if you wish, you may take them with you. I shall have my assistant pack them up for you straightaway. Is there any other way I may help you? Would you like some tea while you wait? No, well, then, shall I have your coachman come in and get the gowns?"

Eleanor shook her head and spoke gently, aware that here was the obstacle that might yet trip her up. "No," she said. "For I do not have my coachman with me. Mama needed him. An urgent message that one of our cousins was ill, and she went to see her at once. I suppose I shouldn't have, but I took the opportunity to beg a friend to leave me here on his way to another appointment. I thought that you could summon a hack for me. Was I wrong?"

Ordinarily Mademoiselle Suzette would not think of allowing a young girl to go home from her establishment in a hack. But it had been a long morning and one that promised further difficulties. At that very moment Mademoiselle Suzette could hear a client's temper tantrum starting in one of her dressing rooms and she wished to attend to that matter before it became worse. Miss Redmond, moreover, had never given Mademoiselle Suzette reason to think of her as sly, so she accepted the girl's explanation, odd as it was, at face value. And so, with far greater ease than Eleanor had expected, she found herself in a hack, with several new gowns packed in boxes on the seat beside her, bound for the coaching inn that handled the traffic to Dover.

That had been the only tricky part. Eleanor had had to allow Mademoiselle Suzette's assistant to direct the driver to her own house, then wait until they had traveled a short way in that direction to get the driver's attention so that he stopped the coach and she could tell him she wanted to go to this particular inn instead. Fortunately he had known which one Eleanor had wanted, although he did look a trifle skeptical at her tale of meeting a brother there. Nevertheless, a promise of double the usual fare and a melting smile had persuaded him to abandon whatever scruples he may have had about doing so.

By early afternoon, Eleanor Redmond found herself on her way to Dover with a newly purchased trunk to hold her gowns. She also had the recommendation of two inns at which she might stay until the following day, when the *Golden Mermaid* was to sail across the channel to Ostend.

The coach was far less well-sprung than the one to which Eleanor was accustomed, but at least she was not forced to ride on the outside with the majority of the passengers. And Eleanor was young enough and in love enough to believe all this a part of a marvelous adventure. To be sure, she had been a trifle startled to discover that the journey was going to cost her four pence for each of the miles to Dover, and that each coachman would expect to receive a shilling for each thirty miles traveled and that even the guard would expect half a crown. As Eleanor had not brought above twenty pounds in ready cash with her, this made a significant dent in her purse. Nevertheless she refused to be daunted.

Nor did Eleanor feel in the least homesick. Within a day or two she would be married. Within a week or two she and Jean-Pierre would be back in England and she would see her family again. Because, once she was married, they couldn't refuse to welcome him, could they?

Over and over again in her head Eleanor rehearsed how she would tell Jean-Pierre the story of her cleverness in getting to Dover with her things. She could not wait to see him and to become the Comtesse de Beauvais, for she had no doubt that Jean-Pierre would marry her posthaste and then all concerns about funds would be ended. Ruthlessly Eleanor Redmond suppressed all doubts and told herself that she was the luckiest girl in England. Meanwhile the coach bounced and jolted its way over the road to Dover. No consideration of propriety troubled her. Love would be enough to overcome all obstacles and trials.

What her traveling companions thought did not trouble Eleanor. She smiled at them amiably and then drifted away into her own reverie. One maternal woman guessed her to be a young bride headed for the Continent to be with her soldier husband, and she sighed in sympathy at the thought. The other woman and the gentleman regarded her with open suspicion. To all three Eleanor was simply indifferent.

On the same road Lydia Milford and her brother, Frederick Leverton, and assorted servants and baggage were also traveling to Dover. They rode, however, in a luxurious, well-sprung coach and made far faster time. Lydia Milford, moreover, had packed for every possible contingency and would have been startled into disbelief had it been suggested to her that she should travel with just one trunk as Miss Redmond was doing. Frederick Leverton, on the other hand, would probably have been relieved at the thought of doing so.

When Lydia suggested, in midafternoon, that perhaps they should send back to London or turn back themselves because she had forgotten a particular batch of neck cloths Jason might want her to bring, Leverton informed her firmly, though with a smile, that if she did so, he would not return with her. Indeed, he went so far as to suggest that if she could not purchase what she wished in Dover, then the matter could not be urgent, and to the devil with what Jason might desire!

Lydia laughed and patted her brother's arm. "Never mind," she said, "I know that I am being absurd and that nothing could matter less than a pile of neck cloths. Just as you know that I am only being this nonsensical because I am such a horrid sailor and dreading this voyage. I never could abide ships. But I simply must see Jason again. And take care of him, for I am persuaded he cannot be looking after himself properly if he is forever traveling about for Wellington."

Leverton hesitated, then said gently, "You must know, Lydia, that it is unlikely Jason will be able to spare much time from his duties to be with you in Brussels. He will be needed at headquarters."

Lydia squeezed her brother's arm. "I do know it. I am not such a nodcock as I must sound just now, but I am so worried about Jason. It is precisely because I do have a strong notion as to the reality of a soldier's life that I am so concerned. He may not be able to spare me much time, but if fighting should come to Brussels and he should be wounded, I want to be near enough to go to him and help nurse him. I've a fair idea how high casualties run when there is no one who cares doing so."

With a frown Leverton said, "Do you mean Jason expects fighting near Brussels? And that he still will let you come? I cannot credit it."

Crossly Lydia tossed her head. "Oh, do stop being so—so brotherly. Of course Jason has not told me he expects fighting near Brussels. Even if it were true, he would scarcely pass me information in a letter that could harm England were it to fall into the wrong hands. No, it is more a sense I have that where Wellington goes, the battles cannot be far behind. Napoleon, Jason has said often, is a man who cannot resist a challenge. And yet you are right that Jason must not expect danger to Brussels or he would have quite forbidden me to come."

And with that she settled more comfortably into her seat.

Perhaps the only traveler who might have been expected to be on the road to Dover and who was not was the Comte de Beauvais. But then perhaps he meant to start out very late and arrive just before the packet sailed. That was certainly what Miss Redmond would have assumed had the information been imparted to her that he still remained in London. Such is the loyalty of young maidens.

4

THE *GOLDEN MERMAID* rocked uncomfortably beneath Miss Redmond's feet as it pulled away from the dock in Dover. She stood at the rail uncertain whether the unfortunate feeling in her stomach was due to the motion of the boat or to lack of sleep. The coach had reached Dover after midnight and her bed at the inn had been damp and uncomfortable, an experience to which Miss Redmond was definitely not accustomed.

The boat rocked again and Miss Redmond clung to the rail wondering, a trifle desperately, why she had not seen Jean-Pierre board the packet for Ostend. He could, of course, have gone on board first, for Eleanor had been late rising. And perhaps he did not wish to show himself until they were out of reach of shore and it was impossible for her parents to stop them. But Miss Redmond could not rid herself of an increasing uneasiness. It was not surprising then that the sensation in Eleanor's stomach grew steadily more distressing.

Just when she was about to turn to go below, a seaman bowed to her and held out a note. "Been asked to gi' it to ye," he said roughly, and then disappeared.

With a hand that only trembled slightly, Eleanor opened the note and gave a gasp of pleasure as she saw that it was signed by Jean-Pierre. So he had not failed her, after all. Pleasure, however, swiftly gave way to dismay as she read the words he had written.

> Mademoiselle Redmond,
> No doubt you are by now en route to Ostend. I hope the sea will not make distress for you. As for me, I shall not be joining you. Ever. Bon voyage, and I hope you like the Continent.
> Jean-Pierre, le Comte de Beauvais

With a sense of desperation Eleanor looked about her, blinking rapidly. The first thing she noticed was the group of gentlemen standing nearby and talking cheerfully. They were also staring at her.

Even as Eleanor stood frozen by the rail, a gentleman wandered over, someone she had often seen with Jean-Pierre. In a voice that seemed to carry only to her ears he said as he passed her, "So Beauvais has won his bet, after all! Convinced the oh-so-lovely Miss Redmond to run away with him, even though he was not at her side. How amused everyone will be to hear the news."

Eleanor would have swayed had pride not held her steady. But she could not refrain from catching her lower lip between her teeth, tears glistening unmistakably in her eyes. With a sinking sensation Eleanor Redmond realized that she had just been publicly ruined, and she wanted nothing so much as to sink into the deck. The deck held firm, however, and instead, she stood with one hand clenched on the railing behind her. As she did so, a gentleman she had not yet noticed moved closer and said with commendable sangfroid, "Ah, Miss Redmond, there you are. My sister is looking for you. Will you come below now?"

In a daze Eleanor looked up at him, recognizing in spite of her blurred vision a gentleman she had seen about town who was now staring at her with a hint of amused sympathy in his eyes. Aware that she was about to dissolve into tears at any moment, and unable to think of any other refuge, Eleanor swayed toward him and said, "Yes. How stupid of me, I seem to be a far poorer sailor than I expected."

"My sister, Lydia, is also a poor sailor, which is why she will be grateful for a fellow sufferer, I am sure," he answered kindly, guiding her half-blind steps to the ladder.

When they were below and Eleanor's eyes had cleared, she looked to see that no one was about, then in a brittle voice she said, "Thank you, sir, for helping me below. You will forgive me, I am sure, for not being able to recollect your name just now. However, as I am equally sure there is no sister, you will understand if I bid you good day right here."

Eleanor turned to go but found herself held instead in an iron grip, the brown eyes still staring at her. The gentlemen's face held a smile, but his words were firm as he said, "Ah, but there is a sister. Her name is Lydia Milford and she really is suffering from seasickness. I do wish you will come and see her right now. If you are sick, you can suffer with her, and if you are not, perhaps you can help."

Tired and nearly undone by the sympathy evident in his face, she was betrayed into replying, "Why do you ask me to?"

The smile still did not leave his face. "Because it is in my mind that we may very well be able to help you, Miss Redmond. And it will be easier if you come with me now."

Eleanor did not ask how he knew her name. It had been, she reflected bitterly, a matter of pride with her that there was not a single gentleman in London who did not know who she was. Instead, Eleanor demanded, in a voice that was not entirely steady, "I cannot think it likely that your sister will wish to help me, sir. Why should either of you?"

Just then the ship lurched and Eleanor found herself in the gentleman's arms, looking up at him.

"Won't you please just come?" he asked gently.

As the gentleman stared down at her, an unexpected warmth in his eyes, Eleanor felt her color rising. In confusion she looked away, afraid he would read her own desire to stay where she was, or even to press her face against his broad chest. Suddenly she wanted nothing so much as to stay in his strong arms, but as they tightened about her, she hastily pulled free. "I don't even know who you are," Eleanor protested, panic in her voice.

The smile still upon his face, the gentleman executed a half-bow in the narrow passageway. "I am Frederick Leverton, Miss Redmond," he said promptly. "And now, unless you wish to become the butt of still more gossip, I suggest we find my sister's cabin."

Eleanor would have protested again, but the sound of approaching footsteps panicked her further. She did not, she realized, have a clear idea of where to find her cabin, nor did she want to be alone just now, in any case. If what she was doing was foolish, it was no more so than her behavior of the past few days, indeed the past few weeks. So, hastily, in a whisper, she said, "Lead the way, sir."

A few minutes later Leverton rapped on the door of his sister's cabin and Lydia called out that he was to go to the devil. With a grin he opened the door anyway and gave Miss Redmond a small push forward. Mrs. Milford lay on her bunk, already pale and clearly in distress. She roused herself sufficiently to say, "I told you to go to the devil, Freddy! How can you possibly think I wish to have company now?"

"Oh, I know you don't want company," Leverton replied cheerfully, "but Miss Redmond does. As well as someone to help her out of a scrape."

As Lydia looked at the girl in patent disbelief, Eleanor colored furiously. "I-I'm sorry," she stammered. "If you want me to go away, I will. I don't want to be a bother, truly I don't."

"Where are your parents?" Lydia asked the girl in ominous accents.

Eleanor looked to Leverton for help. He smiled reassuringly at her, then said, with the same cheerfulness as before, "Well, you see, Lydia, that's the rub. Miss Redmond hasn't got any parents."

"Of course she does," Lydia retorted. "I've met them in London."

"Yes, but that's the trouble," Eleanor said quietly, "they are still in London."

Diverted now, Lydia Milford temporarily forgot

her seasickness. "Then, who are you traveling with?" she asked with avid curiosity.

The ship lurched and Eleanor with it. Leverton helped her into the cabin's one chair, and she accepted his aid gratefully. For one thing, she needed the moment to come to some sort of decision. Some inner sense of prudence warned her not to tell anyone else her trouble, but that warred with the awareness that her only hope to come about was with someone's help. In the end Leverton answered for her. It appeared that he knew more than she had realized.

"I collect Miss Redmond is traveling alone," he said gravely. "If the tales I have heard are correct, then she believed herself to be eloping with the Comte de Beauvais. He, however, was engaged in a wager with some friends—a wager that he could convince Miss Redmond to behave in just such manner despite the fact that he in truth had no desire whatsoever to elope with her."

"Well, where is Beauvais, then?" Lydia demanded.

Coolly Leverton replied, "In London, according to one of his friends who watched us all board the ship."

If it were possible, Eleanor had gone even more pale as she listened to what Leverton had to say. Listlessly she said, "It seems I am more thoroughly ruined than I had feared. And to think it is because I am not eloping with the man I loved, after all."

For the moment the brother and sister ignored her. "But why bring her to me?" Lydia demanded.

Leverton looked down at his boots as he replied, "I thought you might care to help her."

"Me?" Lydia demanded in disbelief.

"Well, it does bring to mind some of the scrapes you got yourself in and out of a few years ago," Frederick said apologetically, a smile twitching at the corners of his mouth. "I thought that if anyone could sympathize with Miss Redmond's plight it would be you."

For a very long moment Lydia Milford was silent. That there was a certain justice in Freddy's words she could not deny. In the end she smiled wanly. "You are right, of course. Dash it all, anyway. Somehow I shall find a way to bring Miss Redmond about. Meanwhile, Miss Redmond, what am I to call you? After all, if we are to convince everyone that we are old family friends and that I am taking you to Brussels to be a companion to me and as a favor to your parents, we must be on other terms than Mrs. Milford and Miss Redmond. You may call me Lydia."

Feeling a trifle dazed, Eleanor said, "My name is Eleanor, but my family has always called me Nora."

"Good. Nora it shall be," Lydia said decisively. She paused as the ship lurched, then managed to go on, "Are your parents to be trusted, my dear? Will they have hushed up your disappearance, or will they have trumpeted it all over London? And did you leave a note for them to find?"

"No note. I meant to send them letters from Dover, but there was no chance," Eleanor replied, her voice scarcely above a whisper. "And they will have done their best to hush it up. But what good is that if Jean-Pierre—the Comte de Beauvais, I mean—tells everyone what occurred?"

Lydia Milford pursed her lips with a secret satisfaction. "My dear Nora," she said, "you and I will be in Brussels, and Beauvais will not. Even if he were, I should enjoy the chance to stare him down. We need only say that his plan failed, but hearing you were to accompany me to Brussels, he was scurrilous enough to try to capitalize on it. If we are still met with skepticism, the solution is merely to stare coolly at the doubter and ask why, after all, if Beauvais were pretending to elope, he would not set you out on the North Road instead of toward Dover and headed for Brussels. Believe me, cool self-assurance will carry us through. And by the time you are back in London some other scandal will have supplanted yours. I do not say it will be easy, but we shall contrive. Now, our first concern must be to send a message to London to reassure your parents and tell them what tale they are to confirm. Freddy, you will arrange for it as soon as we land in Ostend.''

Leverton managed to execute a sketchy bow despite the continued lurching of the ship. And that reminded Lydia of how wretched she felt. ''Oh, do go away now, Freddy,'' she said crossly. ''Though you are welcome to stay, Nora. I can't think where my maid has gone to, unless she is even more unwell than I am. Are you a good sailor, my dear?''

Eleanor did not trust herself to shake her head and instead replied carefully, ''Not very, ma'am. Though this is the first chance I have had to discover it. Do you know, if he had to cross water to do so, I cannot think why Napoleon chose to escape Elba.''

In spite of her condition Lydia Milford laughed delightedly. ''You were quite right, Freddy, I do like Nora! Now be off with you before we disgrace ourselves by being wretchedly ill in front of you, do you hear me?''

With a final grin, Leverton did as he was bid, and the two ladies were able to suffer in private.

5

ELEANOR STEPPED ONSHORE at Ostend with a sense of great relief. She had expected to be terribly depressed by the time they reached the Continent, but she had not counted on the infectious good humor of Lydia Milford or her brother, Frederick Leverton. The winds had soon settled down and so had the waves so that both Eleanor and Lydia had recovered reasonably well before the channel had been crossed. The two ladies quickly became fast friends. Eleanor liked the older woman for her kindness, and Lydia, as Freddy had predicted, felt a nostalgic fondness for a girl as heedless and impetuous as she herself had been at eighteen. And all three could not help but feel a certain satisfaction at the notion of thwarting the Comte de Beauvais.

They still had some distance to travel, however, and Leverton discovered the name of an inn where he would be able to make the necessary arrangements to get them first to Ghent and then to Brussels. He also made sure, before leaving the ship, that the messages written by Miss Redmond and his sister would be delivered to Lord and Lady Redmond as soon as possible.

Other eyes, interested eyes, observed their departure from the ship, and one gentleman remained on board to return to England and report developments to Beauvais.

At the inn Leverton engaged a private parlor for the two ladies and, when they were safely ensconced there, went back out to walk about the town and make the arrangements for their travel.

In the parlor, Lydia Milford removed her bonnet with a sigh of relief. "There," she said with patent satisfaction, "dry land at last! And privacy, so that there are not a hundred men staring at one always. It is fortunate for Jason that I am so much in love with him, otherwise he could whistle for his wife and I would not come."

"Is your husband then in Brussels?" Eleanor asked hesitantly. "Why didn't he just take you with him in the first place?"

For a moment Lydia stared at her young companion, then burst into a merry peal of laughter. "Oh, dear," she said. "In the midst of all this we never did explain, did we? Somehow it seems to have gotten overlooked. My dear Nora, Jason could not take me with him for the very excellent reason that he is an aide-de-camp to Wellington. He is Colonel Jason Milford, and although he was very briefly on leave with me, the moment that wretch Napoleon escaped from his island Jason went back to Wellington's side. And from there he was sent all over Europe. I have only just succeeded in coaxing from him permission to come to Brussels, and I fear that if Napoleon makes a push in that direction Jason will promptly pack me back off to England."

"Wouldn't you want to go?" Eleanor asked curiously. "I mean, wouldn't you be afraid to be near the fighting?"

"Of course I would be afraid," Lydia replied, eyes wide in amazement. "What an absurd question. But what has that to say to the matter? Jason is in Brussels, or will be more often than elsewhere. So what if I am afraid? Must I act on that fear? Men never do. At least not those everyone calls brave. Jason always says that by definition a man cannot be brave unless he was afraid when he did whatever it is he did to be called brave. So I should take a leaf from my husband's book and stay as close as I could to his side so that if he needed me I would be there." She paused, then added fondly, "Not that Jason would see matters that way, but I do."

Watching the older woman, Eleanor felt a pang of something that might have been envy run through her breast. So that was love, she thought. It made what she felt for Beauvais seem like such a pale thing by contrast. She tried to tell herself that Lydia Milford was only being melodramatic, but she had pretended the part too often herself to believe it. No, Eleanor found she could not truly doubt Lydia's sincerity. And that was a most lowering reflection.

Eleanor was still feeling uncharacteristically subdued when Leverton fairly bounced into the room with a cheerful grin upon his face. "Well, I've done it! Engaged a chaise and four for us and another carriage for our baggage and the servants. We leave tomorrow at dawn or as soon thereafter as possible." Seeing the look of disbelief upon their faces, he added, "What's the matter? You don't look at all pleased, and just think of the trouble I've gone to arranging everything."

Lydia turned to Eleanor and said as though her brother were not there, "Don't mind Freddy, Nora. He may talk about dawn, but I shall be much surprised if he is not the last one ready in the morning."

Eleanor laughed. She turned to Leverton and said, a trifle shyly, "You are kind in taking the trouble to arrange for me as well. I must tell you, however, that my funds are . . . are a trifle low just now, but I have asked my parents to forward me some in Brussels."

Leverton merely shrugged. With his head cocked slightly to the side, he looked at his sister as he said, with a wry smile, "Ah, but you need not worry about that, Miss Redmond. My sister is very well to pass and shan't even feel the extra expenditures on your behalf. And since I shall insist that she pay the shot everywhere, there cannot be the slightest impropriety in accepting such a circumstance."

He ducked as his sister's recently removed bonnet sailed past his head, but Eleanor noticed that Lydia was laughing in spite of the way she retorted, "Pig!"

A moment later, however, Lydia was asking her brother seriously, "How did you manage to arrange everything so quickly, Freddy? I should have thought there might be a wait to procure a carriage?"

He hesitated a moment before he replied, the grin gone from his face, "It seems there are a great many nervous Nellies these days in the Lowlands and there are more people headed to Ostend than away to Brussels or Ghent." Seeing the looks on both their faces, he held up a hand and said soothingly, "Now, now, don't be alarmed. So far as I can discover there is no real cause for such an exodus. Merely rumors. Nothing to worry about. And I know how much you want to see Jason, Lydia. But I both promise and threaten that should the situation change and I think us in danger, I shall turn straight around myself and get you ladies back to England even if I must swim there with both of you upon my back."

Neither Eleanor nor Lydia could help laughing at the image conjured up by Freddy's words, and it was in just such a cheerful mood that they sat down to their supper.

In London Lord and Lady Redmond were beside themselves with distress over Eleanor's disappearance. She had been gone, at this point, more than twenty-four hours. For what seemed to her the tenth time, Amanda was called into her father's study to answer both her parents' questions about the matter.

"Now, Amanda," Lord Redmond told his daughter sternly, "this has gone far enough. You really must tell us what you know about Eleanor. Where has she gone and who has she gone with?"

"I don't know," Amanda replied, twisting her hands nervously together. "I've told you that before."

"You don't know?" Lady Redmond repeated in disbelief. "Impossible! Nora confides in you for everything. You cannot deny you know how entangled she has been with the Comte de Beauvais. Nora has always confided in you her absurd notions. How could she not have done so this time?"

"I don't know," Amanda repeated tearfully. "But I swear to you she didn't. She came back from Almack's after I was asleep, and although she seemed remarkably cheerful in the morning, I swear she said nothing to me of her plans. Are you sure she's run away? Are you sure something didn't happen to her? After all, Nora didn't leave a note or anything, did she? Did you ask Jean-Pierre? Or has he left London as well?"

Lady Redmond drew herself to her full height and turned a quelling stare on her daughter. "Jean-Pierre?" she repeated in a frigid voice.

"The Comte de Beauvais," Amanda hastily corrected herself, blushing furiously.

This was too much for Lord Redmond, however. He broke in impatiently. "Yes, yes, I have already been to see Beauvais. He is still in London and so far as I can tell has no intention of leaving the city any time soon. And since I visited him in his apartments, I was able to make sure Nora is not hiding out there. Where she can have gone is beyond me, and if she said nothing to you, I must begin to wonder if something did indeed happen to her."

"Perhaps you ought to question Mr. Braden, Papa," Amanda suggested. "Wasn't he the last one to see her?"

Lord Redmond coughed. "Yes, well, you may be sure Mr. Braden was the first person I spoke with, and he volunteered the information that he left her off at Mademoiselle Suzette's establishment. The poor chap was quite distressed to hear that Nora never returned home; it was all I could do to swear him to secrecy and keep him from setting out to look for her himself."

He paused and Lady Redmond took up the tale.

"Naturally I spoke to Mademoiselle Suzette and she told me that Nora arrived there quite unexpectedly, told a farrago of nonsense that Mademoiselle Suzette somehow believed, and collected some things Suzette had just finished making for her. Then Mademoiselle Suzette put her in a hired hack for home. Impossible, of course, to identify the driver of the hack, but I find it easier to credit that Nora is up to mischief than that the poor fellow abducted her."

"Perhaps Beauvais arranged for him to kidnap her and he is keeping Nora prisoner somewhere against her will," Amanda said with a shiver of delicious anticipation.

"Really, Amanda," Lady Redmond said reprovingly, "your imagination is straight out of the pages of a novel."

"Besides," Lord Redmond added irritably, "I've a man watching Beauvais and he cannot go anywhere without us knowing it."

Amanda was silent a moment, then she sighed, "I suppose you're right. In any event Anna says Nora must have been planning to go because she took her favorite hairbrush with her and her favorite necklace as well as a few other pieces of jewelry."

For a moment Lord and Lady Redmond stared at their daughter in astonishment. Then grimly Lady Redmond said, "I must hope Anna is not as indiscreet with the other servants as she was with you. We told her not to tell anyone."

"Oh, she didn't," Amanda replied blithely. "Not since you called her in here. This was yesterday, when she was helping me pin up my hair before dinner. Anna merely said that it was an odd thing she couldn't find the hairbrush or necklace. And then she shrugged and said no doubt they would turn up later. But of course they didn't, and at bedtime she told me it almost looked as though Nora must have taken them with her and meant to be gone overnight. Today, of course, she wouldn't say a word to me about any of it."

"I see," Lady Redmond said frostily. "Very well, you may go to your room now, Amanda. I am sure I need not tell you how important it is that not a word of Nora's disappearance leaks out."

"What if someone should ask me where she is?" Amanda asked a trifle breathlessly.

Lady Redmond regarded her daughter with eyebrows raised. "My dear girl," she said, "you must simply take care not to give anyone the opportunity to do so."

When Amanda had left the room, Lord Redmond turned to his wife and said with a harassed air, "That's all very well to tell our daughter, my dear, but what do we do if we are asked? Tell the person Eleanor is indisposed? We cannot be certain that no one has seen her out and about."

Lady Redmond considered the matter carefully before she answered. "You are quite right, of course. I think perhaps our better strategy will be to say that she is visiting friends. That way, if anyone saw her on any of the roads or even here in town, that will answer. And once we find out who accompanied her, we can say that it was at our request."

"But which friends?" Lord Redmond moaned, wiping his forehead with his handkerchief. "And what do we say if she was with a man?"

"That," Lady Redmond replied witheringly, "will depend upon where she was seen, of course. Come, there is no great difficulty about it. We must simply cultivate a vague air about the matter until we can discover something certain about Nora's whereabouts."

"Well, I cannot like it," Lord Redmond said fretfully. "I cannot like it at all."

Lady Redmond kissed her husband upon the cheek. "Yes, dear," she said. "This is a dreadful mess we find ourselves in. But we shall come about if only Nora has the sense to keep her wits about her, wherever she may be right now. And I expect she shall. Impetuous the girl may be, but you have never sired a simpleton. You must have faith in yourself as well, for I assure you I most certainly do."

Lord Redmond smiled gratefully at his wife and stroked her hair in return. "My dear, what would I do without you?" he murmured.

Lady Redmond was amused. "No doubt marry a vastly younger, vastly prettier woman and dwell in outrageous scandal with her. You would have the time of your life!"

"Not a bit of it," Lord Redmond retorted fondly. "Though I've no doubt that if something happened to me, you would have no trouble outshining your own daughters with the gentlemen. I wonder you put up with a decrepit old fellow like me."

Arching one eyebrow, Lady Redmond said incredulously, "Decrepit? After what you did with me last night?"

Lord Redmond blushed. "Care to go upstairs and do it again?" he asked, ogling her.

She laughed. "You know very well I should," she said, "if we were not due at Lady Crane's party in an hour. And under the circumstances, I do not think we dare cry off."

"Very well," he replied, shaking a finger at her,

"but I'll still be ready after we return home."

"Oh, after we return home," Lady Redmond said with a smile and a shrug. "That is another matter entirely."

6

BRUSSELS WAS A city crowded with members of the *ton* as well as European aristocracy, and an air of reckless gaiety was everywhere. To be sure, a few nervous persons had packed themselves off back to England as soon as word of Napoleon's successful acceptance in Paris reached the city, but most were so grateful to be able to visit the Continent again that they were determined not to be driven out. Unless, of course, Bonaparte showed signs of pushing this far north. Even then most members of the *ton* were convinced that Wellington would stop him far short of Brussels. And the presence of a garrison of soldiers nearby not only provided an illusion of safety but also made the city attractive for mothers of girls in search of a husband. Or so Lydia explained to Eleanor.

"But you must not be thinking in that direction yourself," Lydia warned her en route to the city. "Too many of these young men will be dead before Napoleon is defeated again, and I should hate to see your heart broken. After the war is over, well, that will be a different matter."

"Come now, Lydia," Leverton interrupted his sister with a twinkling smile. "How can you give Miss Redmond such advice when you yourself are wed to a soldier?"

Huffily Lydia replied, "That is precisely the reason, Freddy. I know what agonies I felt, when the fighting was going on, every time I heard that there had been a battle Jason could have been involved in. And I should hate to see Nora have to go through them as well. Besides, I know very well how dazzling a uniform can be and I simply am warning Nora to look at the man, not what he wears."

"Again, sanguine advice you singularly failed to heed yourself," Frederick pointed out with his habitual grin. "In any event, must you press Miss Redmond to think in terms of marriage? Can she not simply amuse herself for now? I cannot think that at eighteen she must be desperate to be wed. One could hardly call her a confirmed spinster just yet."

Lydia Milford gazed at her brother fondly a moment before she replied, "Yes, but I shall be much surprised if her parents are not pressing her to think in those terms. I have yet to meet a mother who does not. And when one is as impetuous as Nora, one's parents make an extra push to get one wed before one comes to grass completely."

"Lydia!" Frederick remonstrated after noting Eleanor's stricken expression.

The girl's pallor had not gone unseen by Lydia, however, and she took one of Eleanor's hands in hers. Patting it reassuringly, she said to her brother, "Do be still, Freddy. You are quite in the wrong on this. Of course Nora is distressed by what I have just said. But if you think ignoring the truth of the matter is any solution, you are a great nodcock! I am not censuring Nora. Heaven knows I am the last person who would have a right to do so. But having been in her position once, I know that the best thing we can do is to face the situation and deal with it. It is, after all, merely a matter of how one looks at things."

Lydia paused and looked directly at Eleanor. "Now, my dear," she said firmly, "first of all, you are not lost to all propriety and common sense, you are merely high-spirited. You are not an outrageous flirt, you simply have a warm heart and cannot help being drawn to everyone. You are not spoiled, you are simply accustomed to the love and care of everyone around you. But you *will* now grow up."

These last words were spoken in a tone that brooked no denial. Eleanor swallowed hard and then said meekly, "Yes, ma'am."

For once Lydia did not correct her. Instead, she leaned back against the squabs and said quietly, "It's true, you know. All of those things I have just said. No one has taken you in hand and shown you that there are consequences to everything we do. It is a lesson that I had to learn bitterly, almost losing my darling Jason before I did so. I am determined that shall not happen to you."

There was a long silence before Lydia took a deep breath and said, "Enough. Freddy, do tell us, whom have you discovered is still in Brussels? And what are the latest *on-dits* from there? Oh, how I wish women were free to mingle in public rooms as men do, I am so tired of private parlors!"

All innocence, he replied, "Oh, should I not have engaged one for you? You should have told me. At the next stop I shall be glad to be spared the expense."

"Gammon!" she retorted cheerfully. "I said that is what I should like, not what I am so foolish as to do. And now I am still waiting to hear the *on-dits*, and so is Nora."

With a laugh Leverton leaned back and proceeded to tell his sister what she wanted to know, including imparting the information that John Witton, his best friend, was apparently already in Brussels.

"Where he is no doubt busy disapproving all the nonsense going on there," Lydia retorted primly. Then, relenting, she said with a grin that suddenly matched her brother's, "Yes, yes, I know he is a capital fellow and of all people I should know he can be depended upon when needed most. But I'm afraid he always seems to disapprove of me so very much. Not," she added with a laugh, "without cause, of course. Nora, have you ever met John Witton?"

Eleanor frowned. "I'm not sure. He scarcely sounds like the sort of fellow who would have approved of me or formed one of my court, which means, I'm afraid, that I probably wouldn't have paid much attention to him. How old is he?"

"Twenty-six," Leverton said promptly. "Taller and darker than I am. He is handsome and has eyes that can bore right through one when he stares disapprovingly at one's latest escapades. But as Lydia said, a capital fellow and one to be depended upon when needed most. If he will lend his support to you, you are made. Not the highest stickler will dare to give you the cut direct if John Witton gives his approval to you. Perhaps because he has the reputation of being a more prudish fellow even than any of them."

Eleanor looked a trifle frightened as she said warily, "He sounds very formidable. And if what you say is true, how can you hope to persuade him to support me? He would surely be more likely to disapprove of me himself."

Freddy's eyes twinkled unmistakably as he replied, "Yes, well, the impression John gives is not always quite correct. Indeed, I seem to recall one or two of his escapades that are even more shocking than my own. He simply is sufficiently discreet—and clever—that no one ever comes to hear of them."

"Now, that is an ability I should greatly like to master," Eleanor said with a sigh.

Lydia and Frederick laughed. "Never mind," Lydia said. "We have already agreed you are not to dwell upon what has happened but concentrate on the future." She paused, then added with another laugh, "As for persons whose demeanor is deceptive, Freddy, you are a fine one to speak! I don't care how much you affect a silly grin or pretend to think only of your horses and gaming and such. You've as fine a mind as Witton and as strong a character. You simply enjoy having everyone underrate you, I think."

Leverton turned expressive, wide eyes upon his sister as he said in mock protest, "Calumny! Gross calumny that you should say anything is more important than my horses or my pleasures. Next you will be saying I do not worship my tailor!"

Lydia only laughed and shook her head at him. "Don't believe a word of it, Nora," she said. "Freddy is roasting us, as usual." Lydia paused then added, speculatively, "You know, Nora, your parents should have received my note by now. I wonder what they made of it."

That was a question Lord and Lady Redmond

were not quite ready to answer. Indeed, they were discussing the matter even as Lydia spoke. "Brussels?" Lady Redmond protested. "But that's so far away."

"I know it is, my dear," Lord Redmond replied, moving about the room restlessly. "Since it appears, however, that Nora was already on the packet to Ostend when Mrs. Milford discovered her, there really was no other alternative."

"Not if she was to help Nora hush up the scandal," Lady Redmond conceded with a sigh. "And that was, you must admit, extraordinarily kind of her to do for a stranger. Fortunately this dovetails nicely with the things we have been saying for the past two days. Now we need only add—in the strictest confidence, of course—that Nora was feeling overwhelmed with her many suitors, particularly the importunate Comte de Beauvais, and needed a rest from London. When I think of the turn he has served her—"

"Yes, yes, well, we dare not do anything about that," Lord Redmond said hastily. "If I were to call the fellow out, that would only add to our troubles, though I wish to God I could give him a sound thrashing."

Lady Redmond looked at her husband in astonishment. "Why, sir, I never suggested you should call him out. What an absurd notion!"

"Hmmmm," his lordship murmured in agreement. He was silent a moment, then added, "You know I find it dashed ironic that it is Mrs. Milford who has come to our Nora's aid. I mean, after all, the lady's own background cannot be said to be free of blemish. I seem to recall—"

Lady Redmond cut short her husband's ruminations. "You recall just what I do: that Lydia

Milford was one of the wildest young ladies about. But that is all in the past and there has not been a word to say against her since her marriage five years ago. Indeed, she has become a positive pattern card of propriety, thank heavens. Otherwise there would have been little she could do to help Nora."

Lord Redmond coughed. "I wouldn't go so far as to call her a pattern card of propriety, but, yes, she has changed a great deal. What I cannot understand is why she has chosen to help our Nora."

"Depend upon it, Nora reminds her of her own salad days and she is in sympathy with our daughter," Lady Redmond said firmly, "and I can only be grateful this is so." She paused, then added with a grim smile upon her face, "I wonder how Beauvais will take this setback. I have had no less than four of my bosom bows tell me of his wager. Of course I denied it, but now, finally, we have a means to put paid to his scheme."

The subject of Lady Redmond's conjecture was in the highest of spirits. He had no knowledge yet of what was in store for him, he only knew, that contrary to his expectations, Miss Redmond had not returned to London. A pity. He would rather have enjoyed seeing her public humiliation, for if there was one thing the Comte de Beauvais could not abide it was a female as privileged as Eleanor Redmond. The thought of how his mother had been treated by such women when she first came to London was more than he could bear. But this was the first time his dislike had carried him so far, and he was savoring the taste of victory.

His pockets, moreover, were now well-lined, since he had been prudent enough to make a great many wagers on the matter. And it had been such a safe wager, too, since he had never specified a time limit. So long as Miss Redmond was not married, he could always have pleaded for a little longer to work the deed. But he had not needed extra time. The chit had fallen like a ripe plum into his hands. And that was perhaps more gratifying than all the rest. Nor had he had to spend a great deal out of his pocket to woo her. A few trinkets now and again and an expensive trifle or two that he knew her parents would force her to return. That was all. It had been a surprisingly easy conquest.

Whistling, the Comte de Beauvais closed the door of his apartments behind him as he set out for a luncheon with friends at White's. He was going as someone's guest, of course, but one day, one day, he promised himself, he would be a member in his own right.

7

Colonel Milford paced the floor of Wellington's headquarters, his thoughts concerned with more than just Napoleon's whereabouts. He had sent his message to London at the first indication that there might be danger of fighting in the Lowlands, but Colonel Milford could not help worrying that it would arrive too late to stop Lydia from setting out. He paused, then, his lips pressed into a thin line as he considered the other possibility, the possibility that Lydia would have set out in spite of his warning her to stay where she was.

It was perhaps fortunate for his peace of mind that he was called into Wellington's office a few minutes later for an important staff meeting.

Meanwhile, Lydia, Frederick Leverton, and Miss Redmond arrived at the house Colonel Milford had hired for his wife's stay in Brussels. A generally prudent man, he had written to give her the address in case he was not in the city when she arrived. Nor had he canceled the arrangements upon sending her the missive telling her not to come, for he had no confidence that Lydia would not arrive anyway.

Colonel Milford had likewise engaged a staff for his wife, and so she was greeted by a cook, a majordomo, two maids, and a footman when her traveling coach pulled up in front of the neat little house in Brussels.

Frederick Leverton helped his sister and Miss Redmond step out of the coach and then observed with a grin, "If you ever dare to complain that your husband is a pinchpenny, Lydia, I shall throttle you. He has certainly done well by you here."

And so he had. The house was a comfortable one in the most fashionable district of Brussels. The majordomo spoke some English as well as French and Flemish. Even though Lydia's French was impeccable, she appreciated the gesture. Certainly it would make life easier for her maid and Freddy's man.

Taking the corner of her skirt in hand, Lydia mounted the steps and greeted her staff. The footman immediately stepped forward to help with the luggage and direct the two British servants to their quarters. Meanwhile, the cook suggested tea, an offer the two ladies promptly accepted. Leverton was directed to the well-stocked liquor cabinet at the side of the drawing room. Nor did any of the servants so much as blink at Miss Redmond's unexpected presence.

"Your husband is very kind to you," Eleanor could not help blurting out when the servants had left the room.

Lydia smiled. "Yes, he is. Jason spoils me shockingly and I love it. When you look about you for a husband, Nora, I suggest you find someone just the same. It is such a delight to be spoiled this way!"

Freddy laughed. "Don't let my sister fool you,"

he said with a grin. "Jason is scarcely the man to be led about by the nose by any woman, least of all Lydia. As you will see when he appears, my sister dotes on him quite as much as he dotes on her, and spoils him just as outrageously. Why, it is quite enough to turn one's stomach to see the domestic tranquillity that prevails when they are together. Until, that is, Lydia tries to do something outrageous. Then Jason puts his foot down, and everyone listens."

Somewhat timidly Eleanor asked, "Does bringing me here come under the heading of behaving outrageously?"

"Oh, no," Lydia replied tranquilly. "Jason will quite like you and understand why I did so. Besides, if he did cut up stiff about the matter, I could quite rightly point out that it was all Freddy's idea and let him take my brother to task for it. But don't worry, Jason is far more likely to fall into the spirit of things and look around him for some young men to introduce you to."

"Lydia, that is quite enough. You are putting the poor girl to the blush," Freddy scolded his sister, his tone belied by a twinkle in his eyes. "I cannot think there is any great hurry in introducing her about. Perhaps she needs some time to get over Beauvais' desertion of her."

Miss Redmond blushed very prettily but did not speak. Lydia started to answer sharply, but then something in the girl's face made her close her mouth and, after a moment, said meekly, "Yes, Freddy, I've no doubt you are correct. In any event, a quiet introduction to society here will serve Nora better than to pitchfork her into the midst of things, stirring up gossip. There will be enough of that as it is."

"You know, Lydia," Leverton said lightly, "why don't I go and try to find out where Jason is right now? The poor man ought to be warned we are here. And I shall bring him back with me, if I can."

"Would you?" Lydia asked with delight. Holding out her hands to her brother, she said affectionately, "You are the best brother in the world, Freddy, and you spoil me almost as much as Jason does."

"I shall be back by dinnertime, with or without Jason," he promised with a boyish grin.

Then he was gone and Lydia and Eleanor began making plans as to what they would see and do first in Brussels. Beginning, of course, the next day, since there was no way they would leave the house while Freddy might return with Colonel Milford.

Leverton found his quarry with relative ease at military headquarters. Jason was just leaving the staff meeting.

"What are you doing here?" Jason demanded, thumping his brother-in-law on the back in delight.

"I've come to warn you that I've just escorted your wife to Brussels and that you'd best hide away the dancing girls until she's gone," Leverton answered in a mock-conspiratorial voice.

"Where is my brother Philip?" Jason asked. "I thought he was to escort Lydia."

"Didn't you hear from him yet?" Leverton replied, grinning. "His wife gave birth to a baby girl, and for some odd reason the fellow didn't want to leave them just now."

Colonel Milford nodded. "I am pleased it happened while Philip was still at home," he said.

"But this means, I suppose, that Lydia didn't get my message. Or did she insist upon coming anyway?"

Leverton's smile immediately turned to a frown. "There was no message before we left London," he replied. "Why? Are things serious here?"

Jason shrugged and flung himself into the nearest chair, waving Freddy into another. "I don't know yet," he replied. "We heard a few days ago that Napoleon was on the march. Today we are assured he is still in Paris. So far, Brussels seems in no danger, and some would tell you it never will be. But I would feel safer with Lydia in London."

"Shall I take her straight back there?" Leverton asked quietly.

Colonel Milford shook his head and smiled wryly. "Not yet. Only if I'm sure there is danger. I find I'm far too selfish to wish to give up my wife before I've even seen her. Did she like the house? Was she all right on the journey over? I've not forgotten how seasick she gets."

"She was fine, and Miss Redmond has been excellent company for her," Leverton replied, the grin once more upon his face.

"Miss Redmond? Who is she?" Jason asked sharply, with a frown. "Why didn't Lydia write to tell me she was bringing someone with her?"

"It was an, er, rather sudden decision," Leverton said, his eyes twinkling. "Lydia can tell you all about it later. Can you come now and see her?"

"What? Miss Redmond?" Colonel Milford asked, pretending to misunderstand.

"No, your wife, you dolt!" Leverton retorted, grinning once again. "Though I'll warrant you'll find Miss Redmond worth a second glance. She has been this Season's reigning toast in London, you know."

Milford smiled sympathetically at his brother-in-law and read easily the look in his eyes; indeed, it almost seemed as though he could read Freddy's mind. "That way, is it?" he asked. "Pity. I could have told you reigning toasts are not the easiest of ladies to court or fall in love with. As I collect you have. You were used to look just that way and have just that note in your voice with Maria as well."

"Do you think me a fool if I have?" Freddy countered lightly.

"I think you had no more choice in the matter than I did when I fell in love with Lydia," Milford replied. "I also think you had best tell me all about her."

Leverton rose and turned his back upon his brother-in-law. For a long moment he was silent before he said, "How can I explain? Her history you will hear soon enough, and not here, where we may be overheard. As for the girl herself, I had not thought I could be so quickly and easily touched as I was when I first saw her standing alone and about to cry. Then, when I took her hand in mine, it trembled, and I found I wanted to hold the girl in my arms and stroke away her fears. Worse, I found I wanted to capture the sweetness of her lips with my own."

"But you did not," Colonel Milford hazarded.

"No, I did not," Leverton agreed. "I am not such a blackguard as to take advantage of Miss Redmond when she is in my—and Lydia's—care. Indeed, I have taken great care to let her think I see her only as a sort of younger sister. After all, what if she realized how I felt and did not feel the same? The situation would be unbearable for both of us. But I tell you, Jason, it is a devil of a part to play."

He paused and Milford said quietly, "Give me a moment to inform my superiors and I expect I'll find myself with leave to go back to the house with you." Leverton nodded and Milford made an effort to speak lightly as he added, "In spite of rumors to the contrary, Wellington is not a heartless commander, Freddy. Do you know, one of the requisite duties of the unmarried officers in Brussels is to attend the balls and parties and dance with all the ladies? He says it helps morale and keeps up support for our troops. Something necessary, considering how shockingly expensive it is to fight a war these days."

Leverton laughed and waved a hand carelessly. "Take all the time you need. I'm sure my sister and Miss Redmond are only engaging in the most shocking gossip anyway. Tearing our characters to shreds or some such thing."

Colonel Milford laughed as well, then disappeared into another office. Scarcely twenty minutes later he was ready to leave, and the two men headed for the house Jason had hired for his wife.

They arrived to find another guest already comfortably ensconced in a chair by the two ladies and they were all laughing when Colonel Milford and Freddy Leverton entered the drawing room. At the sight of her husband Lydia rose to her feet, ran across the room, and flung herself into Jason's arms. His hug was as fierce as hers, even though, when he finally released her, he said teasingly, "Careful, my dear, or you'll start a scandal! A woman still in love with her own husband!"

"Yes, what an utterly shocking *on-dit*," Lydia agreed cheerfully. Then, pulling on the hand she still held, she added, "Come and meet Miss Eleanor Redmond, Jason. Lord Redmond's daughter. I have fallen into the habit of calling her Nora and she has been the greatest comfort to me on this journey."

Colonel Milford put an arm about his wife's waist as he eyed the girl keenly. Yet aloud he only said, "Then I am sure I shall like her. But aren't you also going to allow me to greet John Witton?"

"Yes, of course, but you and John are already old friends. It is Nora I wish you to be particularly kind to right now," Lydia retorted amiably.

Jason bowed to Eleanor and she curtsied shyly, a gesture that could not help but endear her to the colonel. "We are happy to have you here," he told her gravely. "It is kind of you to keep my wife company."

"Oh, but it is she who has been so kind to me," Eleanor protested, coloring deeply.

Not wishing to embarrass the girl further, Milford turned to his other guest and said cheerfully, "Witton, good to see you again. How do you go on? Already heard about the lovely girl my wife brought with her, eh, and decided to outflank the competition."

A brief smile lit Witton's face, then he replied gravely, "Actually, Miss Redmond was an unexpected bonus. I had only heard that your wife and Freddy were here. How do you go on? Or rather the army? Or shouldn't I ask?" he added, catching the warning glint in Milford's eye. "I keep forgetting how hush-hush all of this is supposed to be. Forget I asked."

Milford smiled, but it did not escape Freddy, who was watching, that the smile did not reach his brother-in-law's eyes. Mentally he began to review the things he might do, should it become necessary to get his sister and Miss Redmond out of Brussels in a hurry. Then, noting Miss Redmond's continued look of distress, he moved to stand beside her and talk quietly about Milford.

Noticing this, Witton said to the colonel, "Now, if you want to talk about a fellow stealing a march upon the competition, you must look to your brother-in-law, Milford."

"Oh, do stop roasting the poor girl," Lydia scolded him with a smile. "And do sit down. You are so tall that you are giving me a stiff neck from having to look up at you. Everyone sit down."

Instead, Witton said, a rare twinkle in his eyes, "I must be going. I know you will forgive me if I take my leave of you, Colonel, Mrs. Milford, Miss Redmond. I only hope you will forgive me for bearing Freddy off as well."

Lydia murmured a polite answer but did not try to stop him. Neither did the colonel.

Freddy met his friend's eyes and also smiled as he said, "I shan't be home to dinner, after all, Lydia." He paused, then added, "John will no doubt be busy introducing me to all the dens of iniquity in Brussels."

"Oh, undoubtedly," Witton retorted cheerfully. "What are friends for?"

Then, with another laugh they were gone and Lydia and Jason Milford looked at each other self-consciously. A twinkle in her own eyes, Lydia said to Eleanor, "Excuse us, my dear, but Jason and I are going upstairs."

"Oh, yes," Milford agreed. "We have so much to, er, talk over, don't we, my love?"

Feeling greatly in sympathy with the pair, Eleanor said quickly, "That will give me a chance to write some letters."

She watched them go and then went over to the writing desk to pen another message to her parents. However much she might have railed at them in the past, she was conscious that in this case it was she who was in the wrong. Biting her lip, Eleanor was also conscious of the need to remind them to send her funds. The small amount she had brought with her would not, she now knew, be sufficient. Already she felt too indebted to her kind hostess, and that could not be allowed to continue.

8

MUCH LATER THAT evening Colonel Milford and Frederick Leverton sat by the fireplace in the small room that passed for a library in the hired house. Both men held glasses of brandy in their hands and were talking quietly. "I didn't see you when you were back in England, Jason," Leverton said with a smile that did not reach his eyes. "My sister kept you all for herself, did she?"

Milford replied to the real question as he said, "My leave was very short, Freddy. In fact, I would not have been in England at all if Wellington hadn't sent me with a private message for certain ears in London. Then Napoleon escaped, and even that little time was cut short and I had to return to Vienna. Lydia and I had not above three days together."

"Tell me about Vienna," Freddy suggested. "Was the congress going well? Before Napoleon left Elba, at any rate?"

The colonel's lips twisted into a wry smile and it was a moment before he answered. And even then he began with an admonition. "What I am about to tell you, Freddy," Colonel Milford said solemnly, "is not to pass beyond these walls. I've no desire to have my career cut short."

Leverton frowned. "If you'd rather not—" he began.

Milford held up a hand. "Peace, halfling. I know you very well. In spite of that careless manner of yours, you've a fine head and I trust you thoroughly. I simply want you to understand the gravity of the matter. Freddy, there is no congress at Vienna."

Leverton all but started up out of his seat. "What?" he demanded incredulously. "But all the countries have delegates there. Wellington himself—"

Colonel Milford cut short his brother-in-law. "All the countries have delegations, true, but there has been no official start of the full congress. One excuse or another has been used to delay matters. You see, Russia, Prussia, Austria, and England all hoped to settle everything between themselves and dictate their decision to the rest of the countries present. But between their own follies, including those of our Lord Castlereagh, and the skill of that devil Talleyrand, everything has dissolved into petty quarreling. We even signed a treaty making England, France, and Austria allies, particularly in the event of a Russian invasion of Europe."

Leverton sat back, stunned, as he tried to absorb this information. "How did this happen?" he asked at last. "And when? Surely Wellington—"

Again Milford interrupted his brother-in-law. "It was Castlereagh's doing," he said bluntly. "As you can imagine, Wellington was less than pleased. But surely you must have heard rumors of it?"

"Yes, but I thought them just that: much exaggerated rumors and the treaty something less sweeping. Something that perhaps just presaged the treaty between England, Russia, Prussia, Austria, and France, not something entirely separate," Leverton replied. "I still wish to know how it happened." He paused, then added, "I suppose part of the trouble began last summer in London? When Prinny and the czar were at such pains to insult each other?"

Milford nodded. "Yes, and the czar's sister did not help. And when you add to it Talleyrand's superb talents as diplomat and mischief-maker, the matter all becomes, if not clear, at any rate understandable. When everyone else spoke of their country's interests, he spoke of justice and legitimacy and public law. In short, Talleyrand claimed for himself and France the ground of high morality, and before it all else gave way. Well, you tell me how likely anyone would have thought it, a year ago, that France would soon be an ally of ours by treaty? I tell you it was unthinkable!"

Colonel Milford paused and added with a smile, "Talleyrand was even as clever in his choice of hostess for the French delegation as he was in everything else. And so much is settled, was settled, or at least discussed at private parties and balls and social fetes. Well, Talleyrand chose his niece, who is as clever as she is beautiful, and as you can imagine, everyone flocked to his affairs."

"And once Napoleon escaped Elba?" Leverton asked with patent curiosity. "How did that alter France's position?"

"Talleyrand made the best of it, as always," Milford retorted with grudging admiration. "He had all along disliked Murat, and when Napoleon escaped, Murat tried to invade the Papal States, and that was the end of *his* power. Wellington, of course, came here as soon as possible after hearing the news. He is certain Napoleon will strike in this direction. At first, I doubted it, but now I begin to believe Wellington is right."

"So Wellington recalled you and you have been kept busy traveling between here and Vienna and all about?" Leverton hazarded cheerfully.

Milford nodded. "It is only in the past two weeks I have been able to settle here."

Leverton set down his empty glass and retorted, "Well, I, for one, am glad you have. In spite of your fears for Lydia, I think she will enjoy being here with you."

"And you?" Milford asked shrewdly. "I'll tell you frankly that I like your Miss Redmond."

A faraway look in his eyes, Leverton replied, "I? I think I may quite enjoy myself in Brussels as well."

With a laugh Milford refilled his brother-in-law's glass. Then he turned sober again as Freddy said quietly, "There have also been rumors about the Princess of Wales."

Milford sighed. "They are true. She has been everywhere outrageous: riding in a shell-shaped phaeton, wearing the most scandalous of bodices, and once, I swear, appearing with half a pumpkin on her head."

"I had hoped the rumors were exaggerated," Freddy replied grimly.

"They are not," Milford replied.

"Can no one stop her?" Freddy asked.

"Our minds are more concerned with Napoleon," Milford said with some asperity, "and it is that which occupies our energies."

* * *

Although many were warned about Napoleon and what his ambitions might mean for England, the concern was not openly spoken of and found, instead, expression in the constant round of balls and fetes and such that people gave so that they would have less time to think. To these the Milfords and Leverton and Miss Redmond were naturally invited.

Indeed, Eleanor found herself a marked favorite, just as she had been in London. There might have been a few matrons who looked at her askance because of the rumors that had reached the city about the Comte de Beauvais. But Lydia Milford's unqualified support of the girl and her husband's position on Wellington's staff kept the tattleboxes relatively quiet and the matrons from snubbing her outright.

In any event, the gentlemen who flocked about Eleanor were inclined to forgive her a great deal, even had the rumor been true. After all, it was not as though she had actually run away with this fellow Beauvais; her virtue must still be intact. But they were also inclined to wonder if she might perhaps allow them liberties. Grimly Eleanor set out to salvage her reputation if she could.

Whatever the evils of her position, Miss Redmond was aware that they might have been far worse. And she was too young and healthy to remain in depressed spirits for very long. Lydia insisted upon lending her funds, against those her parents were sure to send, allowing Eleanor a shopping expedition to acquire some of the delightful clothes and furbelows that she had admired, as well as certain necessities.

Wellington, moreover, set her up, once and for all, by speaking to her kindly at the Mayor of Brussels' ball.

And yet Eleanor found herself thinking that she would have been far happier had Frederick Leverton laughed with her as easily as he did with Lydia and any number of ladies. Only upon her did he ever seem to turn serious eyes, and when he did so, it seemed to Eleanor that her knees grew weak and she found herself turning away, uncertain how to handle these unaccustomed feelings.

Indeed, more than once Eleanor found herself wishing she had her mother there to counsel her. The emotions Frederick Leverton stirred in her breast were at once wonderful and disturbing. Even Beauvais had never made her feel as she did now, wanting by turns nothing so much as to have him speak to her and then nothing so much as to escape his piercing gaze. Something had happened on the boat when he had touched her, and Eleanor still felt shaken to the core.

Back in England, Lord and Lady Redmond had wasted no time in replying suitably by the next post. They also sent a sharply worded missive to their wayward daughter as well as the afore-mentioned draft for funds that should cover her needs until she returned to London. Among the *ton* they made it known that Eleanor had traveled to Brussels in the company of Mrs. Lydia Milford because she had grown bored with the London scene. It was a stroke of genius that Lord and Lady Redmond made no effort to say her decision was anything but a whim.

Such behavior, after all, was sufficiently capricious that it found great credibility with anyone who had known the girl. Particularly with those who were aware of the Comte de Beauvais' wager and who considered it excessively bad *ton*.

"Never did believe the fellow," was a common comment, "much too smoky by half. It's preposterous. Why, what girl would run off and expect the fellow to join her later? Certainly not someone as delicately bred as Miss Redmond."

So, in short order, the Comte de Beauvais found himself in disfavor among the *ton*. His wager, had it been true, would have been bad enough, but to have lied about the results was going much too far. Worse, from Beauvais' viewpoint, was that those gentlemen from whom he had won the wager were now requesting that he return the winnings. Something that was impossible, since the funds were already all but spent. Clearly, desperate measures were going to be required to salvage the situation. Beauvais began to pack for a journey.

9

THE BALLROOM WAS large and drafty and lit with a great many candles. Flowers were heaped everywhere and it was hard to believe that a war might be fought only a short time away. The ladies wore their gayest gowns and some had been so bold as to damp their skirts. Others wore sandals straight from Paris, bought before Napoleon escaped Elba, and feathers in their hair. The men were equally resplendent in their best lace and velvets. Or in uniforms that were immaculately clean, as though their only purpose were to set off the soldier's figure and never to be worn in battle.

Diamonds sparkled everywhere and Eleanor found herself thinking that this brilliant scene made London's Season seem almost flat by comparison. As soon as she arrived, several gentlemen begged her for a dance, and Lydia Milford relinquished her young guest into the charge of a dashing captain of the Guard.

After the young couple was out of earshot, Lydia turned to Leverton and said, "Come, dance with me, Freddy."

"What? Dance with your own brother?"
Leverton feigned shock.

Mischievously Lydia laughed. "Yes. I shall close
my eyes and pretend you are Jason. He was
needed at headquarters tonight. Some message to
carry for the duke, I collect."

Without further argument, Leverton escorted
his sister onto the dance floor and flirted with her
shamelessly to divert her mind. Thus he did not
see the Comte de Beauvais make his entrance.

Eleanor was not so fortunate. She saw Beauvais
the moment he walked through the door. Nor was
she oblivious to the number of eyes that were then
directed at her. So, she thought with a sinking
heart, it would not be as easy as she had hoped to
put her folly behind her.

Fortunately Eleanor's partner appeared
unaware of either the Comte de Beauvais'
entrance or the attention the pair of them were
receiving. Instead, he continued to chatter on
about how splendid it was to be in uniform and
how, should Boney dare to come north, he would
receive a sound thrashing. Eleanor murmured all
that was suitable and meanwhile looked about her
for a chance to escape.

But there was no doing so. Beauvais was not in
the ballroom five minutes before he moved toward
the dance floor and took up a position at its edge,
staring at Eleanor. Aware that he would pursue
her if she tried to evade him, Miss Redmond
squared her shoulders and said to her partner, "I
am very sorry, but I have a slight headache. Could
we sit down?"

"Of course," the young captain said at once, and
led her off the floor.

It was a calculated gamble. Interested eyes

would note that she had not stayed the whole dance, but they would also see that she made no effort to evade the count. Fewer ears, moreover, would hear the scene that Beauvais most evidently intended to create.

Eleanor was correct. She had scarcely stepped off the dance floor before Beauvais was bowing in front of her and taking her hand in his. "*Ma chère*," he said, raising the hand to his lips. "Why did you not wait for me in Dover as you swore you would when we conspired to run away together? I was desolate to arrive and discover you gone. Why did you desert me?"

Miss Redmond was not, in general, a very good liar. But anger made her eyes sparkle and her voice firm as she replied icily, "Monsieur, I have no idea what you are talking about. I came to Brussels with Lydia Milford and arrived to discover that there was some absurd rumor that I had made plans to run away with you. I gave you credit, sir, for having had no part in spreading such a calumny. But it seems I was mistaken." Eleanor paused and forced herself to laugh before she added, "Monsieur, the notion that I would choose to run away with you is absurd!"

But the Comte de Beauvais was equally clever. "*Ma chère*," he said, "you are angry with me. You feel I failed you by arriving too late to be on the boat with you. A thousand apologies, but please, please do not believe I meant to desert you," Beauvais went on, still holding on to her hand. "My love for you is as strong as ever."

Without haste Eleanor pulled her hand free. Frostily she replied, "And mine for you is as non-existent as ever."

The captain of the Guard had been standing

beside Eleanor stunned into silence by the count's words. He now came to her defense. "Sir, you are distressing the lady," he said coldly to Beauvais.

Beauvais grew very still. The dance had ended and more people were gathering around the pair, interested to hear what would be said next. It was now that Frederick Leverton and his sister became aware of the count's arrival.

"You spoke very differently in London, *ma chère*," Beauvais told Eleanor with something of a sneer.

She turned rather pale, but before she could answer, someone else did so for her. In a deprecating voice Leverton said, "Come now, Beauvais, is it really credible that someone who speaks as cruelly and as crudely as you do could have persuaded Miss Redmond to run away with you?"

With eyes flashing daggers of rage, the count turned to the newcomer and said from between clenched teeth, "Who are you to speak to this matter?"

Leverton bowed and smiled his habitual grin. With a shrug he said lightly, "Why, my name is Frederick Leverton, and since Miss Redmond is here in Brussels at the request of my sister, Mrs. Milford, I believe I may be said to have some knowledge of the matter." He paused, then added in the same careless voice, "One might well wonder if you learned of her plans to travel with my sister and used that knowledge to place the extraordinarily unsavory wager that one has heard tell of."

The Comte de Beauvais went first pale then red. Particularly when Leverton added, still with a smile, "Of course, one would not wish to believe you had made such a wager at all, since it would be beyond the capability of any true gentleman to do so."

For a moment matters hung in the balance and more than one person wondered if they were witnessing the prelude to a duel. But then the count bowed. "*Touché*," he said softly. "Mademoiselle Redmond is fortunate in her friends. I wonder, though, how it is that your sister came to invite Miss Redmond to accompany her. Perhaps you had some say in the matter?"

Lydia placed a warning hand on Leverton's arm. It was not needed, however, and he was considering just how to reply when someone else did so for him. John Witton, who had joined the group clustered around Beauvais and Eleanor, laughed briefly.

"Why, as to that," he said, "everyone knows Freddy has admired Miss Redmond for some time. But as it is not in his nature to form one of a court, he used rather subtler means to be close to her. Frankly, I think Wellington should acquire his services as a tactician."

That brought a round of laughter, which the count reluctantly joined. As did Freddy. Miss Redmond blushed, a becoming gesture not lost on those around her. With a deceptive smile Beauvais declared himself routed and moved away. His eyes twinkling, Leverton turned to Witton and said, "Now, why the devil must you give away all my secrets, old fellow? Trying to steal your own march, perhaps?"

That brought another round of laughter as Witton replied gravely, "But of course."

"Very well," Leverton said with a graceful wave of his hand. "To show you how magnanimous I am, I shall even make way for you to have the next dance with Miss Redmond.''

Witton bowed, falling easily into the game as he replied, a hint of a smile upon his own face, ''Be sure I shall not waste my opportunity. Miss Redmond?''

Eleanor gratefully nodded and moved onto the dance floor with her rescuer. When they were out of earshot of the others, she said quietly, ''Thank you, Mr. Witton.''

He smiled down at her with all the appearance of a man half-smitten with a lady. ''You are welcome. Though it is Freddy's quick wit we must thank, you know.''

''Nevertheless, thank you for your part in all this,'' Eleanor said warmly.

Witton smiled wryly, then added, ''I do not like the Comte de Beauvais, and like Freddy, I rather enjoyed thrusting a spoke in his wheel. I cannot think what ever possessed you to trust him.''

''Nor can I,'' Eleanor admitted with a grimace. ''Or why, even though I did trust him, I was ever mad enough to agree to his horrid scheme.''

''Because you are naïve, no doubt,'' Witton replied matter-of-factly. Eleanor's eyes opened wide in astonishment. ''Careful,'' Witton admonished her, ''there are a great many eyes upon you just now, and you want to appear to be dazzling me.'' Then, with a smile that astonished her even more, he said, ''Did you think I should not say that to you? Even if I happen to believe it to be true? I don't hold it against you, you know. It is your parents' fault if they did not have the sense to raise you properly. Indeed, it is all the rage to raise one's daughters to be naïve and lacking in common sense, it seems, and never mind that a better prescription for disaster could not exist. Fortunately, you appear to have sufficient wits, Miss Redmond, to remedy the matter yourself."

"How?" Eleanor asked uncertainly.

Witton looked down at her for a long moment, then shook his head. "No. It is a tempting notion, but I shall not try to tell you what to do. How can I? It is for you to discover what does and does not suit you. And in any event, I suspect Mrs. Milford could advise you better than myself."

As the waltz was ending then, Eleanor had no time or desire to reply as Witton relinquished her to her clamoring suitors. Leverton was not among them, and Witton calmly sought out his friend. "Shouldn't you be with Miss Redmond?" Witton asked quietly.

Leverton laughed and his eyes were dancing as he replied, "It has been expressed to me quite strongly that my behavior in pursuing Miss Redmond while she is a guest under my sister's roof is grossly improper. Quite shocking, in fact. That is the decided opinion of any number of dowagers present. And gentlemen. I rather meekly submitted to their scoldings and took myself off to brood while Miss Redmond is allowed the freedom she deserves to pursue her interest in other fellows. I am an unfeeling dog and this is the only way, after all, I can redeem myself at this point."

Witton's own eyes were twinkling as he replied gravely, "Such a badly behaved boy you have been! And such a clever one. I wonder if your scheme to bring her off safely would have been as convincing if Miss Redmond were not an heiress? Fortunately for her, Beauvais' tastes run so strongly elsewhere that even that was not adequate inducement to cause him to actually elope with the girl."

"Deucedly fortunate," Leverton agreed grimly. The look in his eyes at that moment was sufficiently dark that anyone seeing him look at Miss Redmond that way would have been convinced that he cherished a *tendre* for her.

Witton, however, thought he knew his friend too well to be so deluded. "What will you do when this scandal has blown over?" he asked quietly. "Have a falling-out with the girl so that she can safely return to her family?"

Leverton turned brooding eyes upon his friend. In a voice no one else could hear he said, "On the contrary. When all this has blown over, I mean to marry Miss Redmond. If she will have me."

Witton's eyes opened wide. "The devil you say!" he exclaimed.

Once more Leverton's eyes began to dance. "No, no," he protested, "angel, not devil. Miss Redmond is an angel."

"And you," Witton replied calmly, "are a madman."

10

THE DAYS THAT followed were difficult ones for Miss Redmond. It was not to be expected that everyone would believe the tale she and Leverton and the Milfords had set about. There were too many mamas of hopeful daughters who envied her success, and too many visitors from London who recalled her heedless behavior there as well as the awkwardness when she first disappeared, for the story of a supposed elopement to die away. Particularly when the Comte de Beauvais made every effort to revive it.

Lydia Milford was too wise to allow her protégée to hide away, so Eleanor was forced to endure the daily snubs of those who believed Beauvais. The knowledge that his story was the truth was, moreover, a lowering reflection.

There were, of course, supporters who rallied to Miss Redmond's side. But as these were almost all young, handsome, eligible gentlemen or members of the various guards, it could not be said to help her cause with the female members of Brussels' society.

Eleanor felt more than once the desire to flee the censuring tongues. But as the days advanced into June, the rumors of war grew steadily more alarming, and while her escapade was not forgotten, it was supplanted by conjectures over Bonaparte's plans. A number of families fled the Continent, but Lydia and her brother were determined to stay. Eleanor stayed as well. Lord and Lady Redmond had made it quite plain in their letters that they were not eager to deal with such a horridly behaved daughter any time soon and that they were delighted she was where she was. They also wrote that the gossip in London was no better than in Brussels. Worse, in fact, as families returning from the Continent reported Beauvais' continued pursuit of their daughter.

It was a pointed pursuit. Whenever he saw her, the count would bow and greet Eleanor in the most familiar of terms. When she snubbed him, as she always did, he turned it off with a laugh and a joke as to the fickleness of females. He particularly enjoyed doing so at parties when Eleanor was surrounded by other guests and she could not speak frankly to him without causing even more talk. He never persisted more than a few moments —just long enough to overset Eleanor's composure.

So unpleasant had the situation become that Lord and Lady Redmond had even, in their last letter, asked if Eleanor might not consider marriage to Beauvais. Forgotten was their dislike of the man. Forgotten was the fact that he had never intended to marry her. Their only concern was to stop the gossip.

When Eleanor complained bitterly of this fact to her hostess, Lydia replied gently but firmly,

"Well, yes, I know it must be distressing to you, Nora. And it must seem that your parents care nothing for your feelings. But consider. Even they do not know the whole of the matter. They wish only to end the gossip because they know you cannot help but feel distressed by it. And they know that you must have believed yourself in love with Beauvais in London or you would never have acted as you did. Perhaps they still believe you love him and think they are doing you a kindness in giving their consent. Convict them of false presumptions if you wish, but not heartlessness, my dear, for that I will not allow."

"I suppose that, as usual, you are right," Eleanor agreed with a sigh.

"What? My sister usually right?" Leverton said with mock amazement as he entered the drawing room just then. "Occasionally, perhaps, but usually?"

"Oh, Freddy, you are absurd," his sister said indulgently. "Where have you been?"

"With your husband," he replied, carelessly throwing himself into a nearby chair. "Out looking at the roads and troops and such."

Lydia, however, was not deceived by his casual tone. "He doesn't meant to try to send me back to London, does he?" she all but growled. "For, I tell you plainly, I won't go."

Freddy smiled at his sister. "I assure you, Lydia, Jason knows just how stubborn and unreasonable you always are, and he would not dream of asking the impossible of me. No, no, he was just showing me what the situation is and advising the best roads to take, should his troops need to retreat past Brussels and you wish to follow."

"Gammon!" Lydia retorted sharply. "But I must

say I am grateful you are here to lend us your support, should the worst occur. I cannot believe that Wellington will allow the French to best him, but one cannot be as certain about the Prussian or local troops. They are, after all, not ours."

Leverton laughed. "Mere prejudice, I assure you," he said, though he knew there was a certain justice to her words. "In any event, their commanders have placed themselves in Wellington's hands. If the duke has a concern, it is that so many of his veterans were sent to America after Boney was captured and there has been no time to call them back. British or not, too many of the troops are raw recruits, as yet untested. And that is the circumstance none of us can like."

For a long moment the three sat in sober silence. Finally Eleanor said, "Is there anything we ladies can do to help?"

"If the battle comes to Brussels," Leverton replied gravely, "every hand will be needed to help nurse the wounded or at least prepare bandages and such. Then the ladies—and we idle gentlemen —will come into our own. If you cannot help with the nursing, Miss Redmond—and I assure you no one will expect you to—you can help prepare bandages and locate pillows, blankets, that sort of thing. But for now we can only wait and try not to get in Wellington's way. I think the thing he most despises is all of the advice given so freely by those gentlemen and ladies who have never in their lives faced a battle."

"How strange to think of Wellington so, though Jason has said the same thing," Lydia mused slowly. "At balls and parties he seems so carefree and confident and ready to listen to everyone. He poohs the danger of fighting reaching this far north and laughs at the thought that Napoleon's men might be a match for ours. Yet Jason says that in private his spoken sentiments are far less sanguine."

She shivered and Leverton moved closer to pat his sister's hand reassuringly. "Never doubt that Wellington knows what he is about," he told her. "Whatever he says and to whomever he says it, he has a reason. And you must admit that a populace in panic could scarcely help the morale of the troops. Not to mention that roads clogged with fleeing families would mean that supplies would have greater difficulty getting through."

"Well, I wouldn't mind if the Comte de Beauvais panicked and went back to England," Eleanor said forcefully. "I cannot bear seeing his face all the time."

Leverton grinned at her. "Bear in mind, Miss Redmond, that he is surely no more pleased to have to look at yours regarding him with such disdain. Indeed, sometimes I feel quite sorry for the fellow."

"Sorry for him?" Eleanor demanded, eyes flashing. "How can you say that?"

Leverton regarded his sister's guest with unconcealed amusement. "Well, you must admit it cannot be pleasant for him to have half the *ton* regard him as an unprincipled blackguard who took advantage of an innocent trip of yours to profit on an appalling wager. The other half consider him to be an unprincipled blackguard who caused an innocent young girl to all but ruin herself."

"And yet he is everywhere received," Eleanor retorted bitterly, "while I am given the cut by any number of respectable matrons."

Leverton shrugged. "It is not fair, I agree. But, then, I should have thought you far too intelligent to believe that life is always fair. The Comte de Beauvais is a man—and an eligible one, of sorts—and therefore will be accorded a welcome most everywhere. At the moment he is penniless. But should Bonaparte be defeated once and for all, it is possible he will be able to return to France and retrieve at least some of the family fortune, as he was trying to do when Napoleon escaped from Elba. Then he will be most eligible, indeed. That is how society functions. Approve or disapprove all you like, it changes nothing."

"Oh, how I wish I were a man!" Eleanor told him roundly.

Leverton watched her rise and pace about the room, amusement evident upon his face. "What a pity that would be," he said with an exaggerated sigh. "You would then be unable to break so many male hearts."

"Yes, but she would undoubtedly make a handsome male and break a great many female hearts," Lydia countered cheerfully.

Eleanor turned on them both and said, "How can you talk such nonsense? As though I cared about such things? As though they mattered?"

Without haste Leverton rose to his feet and crossed the room to Miss Redmond. Immediately, in confusion, she turned away from him. Gently Freddy placed his hands on her shoulders and turned her back to face him. His ready smile was tempered by the genuine sympathy in his eyes as he said, "I am sorry for roasting you so. But can you really blame us for thinking you lived for just such success? In London you did not appear to disdain admiration. Indeed, you were infamous for your heartlessness in ensnaring the affections of young gentlemen and then quite casting them away."

Eleanor trembled beneath his touch and it was all she could do not to sway toward him as she said, "It didn't seem that way to me. But in any case, must you throw that up at me?" she demanded, close to tears.

Warmth appeared in Leverton's own eyes and for a moment it seemed as though he would lean toward her. But with an effort he said carelessly, "Am I to be blind to such things?"

"You would be if you were a gentleman," Eleanor replied with lowered lashes.

Leverton could feel her still trembling, and taking a deep breath, he thrust her away from him and ran a hand through his curly brown hair. Forcing himself to laugh, he said, "If I were a gentleman, my thoughts would go unspoken, but I assure you they would be there just the same. Unless, of course, I was a green youth besotted out of my mind with love for you. And I am no longer a green youth."

The warmth in his eyes made Eleanor a trifle breathless as she replied, "And I am no longer the shallow girl who delighted in her conquests in London."

What might have happened next no one can say because Lydia judged matters had gone too far already. Hastily she intervened to say, "That is quite enough, I should think."

Then, tears beginning to spill from her eyes, Eleanor fled the room. When the girl was gone, Lydia Milford looked at her brother and said reprovingly, "What the devil are you playing at, Freddy? You must realize Nora is not the girl to behave toward so outrageously. Were you flirting with her? If so, I must say you went about it very oddly."

Leverton regarded his sister with outrage. "Flirting?" he demanded furiously. "Is that what you really think I was about? I thought that you at least would understand I am more than half in love with the girl and trying very hard not to forget she is your guest."

"And what has that to say to the matter?" Lydia asked naïvely.

Freddy took a deep breath and tried to speak calmly. "Miss Redmond is an heiress and a beauty and by rights ought to marry well. And, meanwhile, to enjoy her successes. Who am I to take advantage of her presence here, as your guest, to press my attentions upon her?"

"Then what were you doing just now?" Lydia asked mildly.

Leverton ran an exasperated hand through his hair again as he replied, "Trying to shake some sense into the girl. Some sense into me as well, perhaps."

"Perhaps you mistake Nora," Lydia suggested mildly. "Certainly in the past few weeks I have seen little evidence that she is the giddy social butterfly you seem to think she must be. Instead, I have seen her go out of her way to talk to a girl who sat by herself at a dance and coax a partner to dance with that girl instead of herself. More than once she has offered to do this or that about the house to help me, and it is Nora who first noticed that the upstairs maid was distressed and discovered her mother was ill. That does not seem to me like a girl who cares more about her social success than the music of her own heart."

Freddy did not at once reply and in astonishment Lydia looked at her brother. Slowly she said, "You really have lost your heart this time, haven't you? I had not thought it possible."

"Why not?" Leverton asked her, his eyes now twinkling. "Because I am always laughing, always flirting with one woman then another? Did you think me capable of nothing more lasting than that?"

"No," Lydia replied frankly. "I thought you hurt far too deeply after the affair with Maria years ago. You once swore that while you would eventually marry, it would be for an heir and not out of some mistaken emotion called love."

Leverton grinned at his sister. "And am I not allowed to change? It has been, after all, seven years since I was that callow boy in love with Maria."

"So it has," Lydia replied coolly. "And if you have, I am very glad for it. I think I should like Nora as a sister-in-law."

It is unfortunate that the subject of this conversation could not overhear it. If she had, perhaps some of what later occurred might have been prevented.

11

THE DUCHESS OF Richmond's ball was an event looked forward to by everyone in the *ton* in Brussels. At any time they would have been happy for invitations to attend, but with rumors that Bonaparte was marching north, people had an added reason to be present. The Duke of Wellington would be there. It was an open secret that the duchess had asked Wellington if she ought to cancel her ball and that he had said she should not. Did that mean the rumors about Bonaparte were wrong?

Few people guessed that Wellington had already given orders to his troops on the field and that now he was concerned with the officers still in Brussels. Who would have realized that he saw the ball as the perfect camouflage for giving orders, knowing full well that all his British officers, including Colonel Milford, would be there?

Nevertheless, nerves were taut as the *ton* set out for the ball. Certainly they were not disappointed in what they found. The Duchess of Richmond had gone to a great deal of trouble to transform her ballroom. The hangings and draperies were in the royal colors: crimson, gold, and black. Pillars were wreathed in ribbons, leaves, and flowers to set off the rose-trellised wallpaper.

There were those who had accused Eleanor Redmond of having given herself over to feverish gaiety, but her behavior was as nothing when compared to many present at the Duchess of Richmond's ball. Perhaps it was the fear that soon there would be war that made everyone so determined to pretend nothing was amiss. A hint of desperation glittered in far too many eyes and too many voices tittered with laughter far too often.

The Milford party had not been at the ball long before Jason disappeared, telling Lydia he needed a word with some fellow officers. Leverton, left to entertain his sister, told her in a quiet voice, "I think we had best make an early evening of it. I don't like the mood of these people, and it cannot help but prey upon Miss Redmond's sensibilities."

Lydia looked about her and nodded. "I shan't mind," she said, then swallowed. "And don't worry about convincing Nora. When we are ready to leave, I shall simply tell her that with Jason about to be called to the field I have no taste for amusement. She will not protest. But do let us give her more time to dance, Freddy. God knows there may be little enough of that in the days to come."

"Poor Miss Redmond," Leverton said, smiling down at his sister. "Am I really such an ogre, cutting short everyone's pleasure?"

"No, you are an angel who takes very good care of us," Lydia retorted fondly, patting her brother's cheek.

In the end they stayed longer than they had intended. Wellington was of course the most eagerly awaited guest, for the Milfords as well as for everyone else, and he did not arrive until after midnight. His conversation was light, but scarcely anyone was deceived and even Colonel Milford had difficulty concealing from those who asked him the gravity of the situation. Indeed, how could it be otherwise when Wellington admitted to Georgiana Lennox that he expected the troops to march in the morning? And how could anyone ignore the dispatch brought in by Lieutenant Henry Webster for the Prince of Orange?

Earlier, dressing at the house, the Milfords had held a conversation repeated in a great many homes that night. Lydia had turned to her husband and said quietly, "Do you wish me to remove from Brussels?"

"You don't want to, do you?" Jason replied with a wry smile.

"No. But I shan't add to your worries by staying if you tell me not to," Lydia replied.

"And if I say you may stay?" Jason asked, cocking his head to one side.

"Then I shall help with the preparations to care for the wounded," she said, tranquilly continuing to dress.

"And your guest? Miss Redmond?" Jason asked. "Is she likely to give way to the vapors if she stays? I shouldn't like you to be burdened with a hysterical female if the fighting should come too close to town."

Lydia shook her head in exasperation. "I wish you will stop crediting Nora with so little spirit or character. It is just like men! They see a girl who is beautiful and popular and write her off as a shallow creature, good for nothing more than decoration. No, Jason, you need not worry about

Nora. She has already told me she thinks we ought to be rolling bandages or gathering pillows and blankets for the wounded. And stockpiling whatever medicines we can in the event they are needed to nurse the wounded.''

Jason winced, then bowed and replied, ''My apologies. And I am glad to hear Miss Redmond will be such a support to you.''

''Then we may stay?'' Lydia asked a trifle anxiously.

He nodded. ''I think I would worry more if you were caught up in some mad exodus to Antwerp. I cannot help but feel you will be safer here, Lydia,'' he replied. ''But, mind, you are to be ready to leave at a moment's notice from Freddy if things go against us. Somehow I will contrive to send him word if they do. Now, we must go to the Duchess of Richmond's ball and smile as though we have not a care in the world. Can you do it, my love?''

''Anything, if you wish it,'' Lydia replied, looking up at her husband with a smile that made him want to embrace her.

Eleanor, though no one had spoken as frankly to her about the situation, was aware of how matters stood. She laughed as gaily as ever and had taken as great pains with her toilette. A gown of silver net over pale-blue gauze with blue slippers and gloves were complemented by sapphires at her throat and ears. In flying to the coast Eleanor had meant to be practical in bringing her best jewels. That way, if the need arose, she would have something to sell. Until now she had kept them put away, knowing that her mama considered her still young to be wearing them and that they had been purchased for her with an eye to the future. But tonight seemed a night to defy prudence and be at one's gayest. And so she laughed and danced and flirted madly with everyone, and if at times her mask slipped and there was a glint of fear in her eyes, no one but Freddy Leverton saw it, and Eleanor avoided his company, conscious of the way his touch had shaken her earlier in the day.

In any event, all eyes and ears were directed toward the military men present. Everyone watched them for some sign that a battle was imminent. Everyone begged them for some crumb of information. Wellington denied concern, but as has been said before, he did not try to hide that something was afoot. And when the dispatches continued to arrive and one by one the officers began to slip away, gaiety gave way to a quiet sobriety and guests began to call for their carriages as well.

Colonel Milford was one of the first to go. He took leave of Lydia with a warm embrace, oblivious of any eyes that might be watching. On the eve of battle a man gives not a damn about what gossips might say.

Soon after that, Freddy came up to Eleanor and said quietly, "The carriage is here and Lydia has no taste for further dancing."

"Of course," Eleanor agreed at once.

Outside, they found John Witton standing by the carriage and he helped to hand in the ladies, then climbed in himself. "Jason asked that John come and stay with us," Lydia told Eleanor calmly.

Miss Redmond swallowed and nodded. "In the event Brussels must be evacuated, I expect he felt it would be good for us to have another male at hand."

Witton gave one of his rare smiles and said, "Oh, Milford spoke no such defeatist talk to me. He merely said that he should feel better were I in the house to help Freddy defend it. Not against the French, as might be expected, but against possible blackguards who would take advantage of any confusion to attempt to loot where they can."

"John is a first-rate shot," Leverton confided to Eleanor, "and any looters had best beware." Then, aware that Miss Redmond had begun to tremble, he went on in a bantering tone, "Not that I expect trouble. I think Jason invited him to stay with us because he thinks John is in need of reassurance. Practically afraid of his own shadow, the man is."

"No, no, it is you who are the coward," Witton took up the bantering easily. "Why, Miss Redmond, I vow it is Freddy who hides under the bed at the sound of thunder."

In spite of herself Eleanor laughed and some of her fear left her. "Gammon," she said roundly. "I don't doubt of either of you being excessively brave. It is we ladies who are terrified, and you know it."

Lydia leaned forward. "I told Jason you did not wish to leave Brussels, my dear, but if I was mistaken, I wish you will tell me now. Freddy could easily have you in Antwerp and over to England in no time at all."

Eleanor took the hand offered to her and said, her eyes beginning to dance, "What? And desert you? A fine thanks that would be for your kindness to me. No, I shall be all right. And if the fighting does come close to Brussels, we will be needed, for I cannot believe there are enough surgeons and nurses to tend to the wounded.

There will be need of anyone who does not faint at the sight of blood."

Startled, Witton said, "Do you mean to nurse the wounded, Miss Redmond? I know that Freddy has said his sister intended to do so, but it is not generally the thing, you know."

Eleanor met his eyes squarely. "War is not the thing, Mr. Witton. And it is madness to think that propriety must be observed at a time like this. I have heard that we have more than fifty thousand men massed to fight. And that Napoleon is marching north with almost twice that many. Nor do I except the Prussians and local men. In a battle that engages so many soldiers there will be confusion and death and horror. The wounded must be evacuated somewhere and I cannot help but believe it will be here."

"But for such a delicately bred young lady—" John Witton began.

Impatiently Eleanor cut him short. "I am no hot-house flower, sir. I have young brothers and I have helped to bandage scraped knees and all the other usual bloody wounds of boyhood. I don't doubt that this will be infinitely worse, but I do not mean to flinch from it."

Lydia nodded approvingly and Leverton took up the bantering again as he said, "You see, John? You are routed already and the French are not even at the door! If worse comes to worst, I see I shall be best put to give your pistsol to Miss Redmond and let her defend the house."

"Oh, no!" Eleanor retorted, as her eyes began to dance. "I shall be hiding under my bed, thank you very much, and shall depend upon both of you for my safety."

"Confess," Freddy said with a laugh. "What you

are not saying is that you find that a most frightening thought."

Eleanor did not answer but tossed her head in reproof.

Lydia turned to Witton. "It is a sadly unbridled house you are coming to," she said. "I wonder you do not dread it. But as you are coming, it occurs to me that someone ought to tell you that you are genuinely welcome. And as soon as we are there I shall have the housekeeper have a room prepared for you."

"Thank you," Witton replied gravely. "I shall send a note to my man to bring my things and pay my shot where I am lodging." He paused, then added dryly, "Colonel Milford appears to believe we may be some time in waiting a resolution of events."

The Comte de Beauvais was equally on edge and for once had no thought of Miss Redmond. His fortune was about to be decided on the battlefield. Should the French be victorious, he must flee back to England and give up hope of ever regaining his inheritance. If his countrymen lost, then he could again return to his homeland and try to regain his estates. In the months Napoleon had been on Elba Beauvais had gone a long way toward convincing the necessary officials to restore his inheritance to him. But when Napoleon marched on Paris and took the city, the count had fled to England to wait. Now, once more, he prayed for Bonaparte's defeat. If that were to come, he would not need Miss Redmond or the money his wager had won him. He could return to France, claim his inheritance, and live as he wished. That was what he hoped for.

A prudent man, he had already arranged to hire horses in the event of a battle. Either way, he was prepared to travel and would not be caught up in the hysteria that was sure to engulf the city of Brussels.

Then, briefly, the Comte de Beauvais did think of Miss Redmond. Should he leave the city, his last act would be to spread about the letters she had been so foolish and impetuous to write him. My, but the girl had a fondness for the pen and absolutely no discretion. Beauvais had assured her, of course, that he had burned the letters the moment they were read so that she need not fear compromise. That no doubt had contributed to her openness. But if she had believed him then, she was even more a fool than he had thought and she deserved everything she got. Miss Redmond would learn a great lesson about trifling with the affections of men.

This thought of revenge for the humiliation she had caused him was followed by a far more practical one. Miss Redmond was an heiress. Beauvais knew from what she had told him that her pin money was very generous and that she could easily obtain more from Lord and Lady Redmond. Stroking his chin as he regarded himself in the mirror, Beauvais considered the matter carefully.

In London he might have needed to fear retribution from her family if he tried to blackmail her, but here in Brussels she could not have such protectors. Indeed, the only possible person she could turn to would be Mr. Leverton. Colonel Milford was about to be embroiled in battle and Mrs. Milford could do nothing. So it would be up to Leverton. But what girl would turn to one suitor to help her when the situation involved billets-doux written to another? No, the more the count reflected upon the matter, the more certain he was that Miss Redmond would have no choice but to pay him not to show the letters about. No doubt she would want them returned to her, but he was confident he could obtain a large sum from her before handing over the things.

Money was a luxury never to be spurned and certainly it would be more comfortable to return to France with something in his pockets. Clapping his hands on his knees, the Comte de Beauvais was decided. Tomorrow or the next day Miss Redmond would receive a note reminding her of the existence of the letters. She would be given another day or so to fret about the matter and then would come his demands. Handled right, she might even believe that it was she who suggested paying him to have them returned.

Smiling, Beauvais sought his bed.

12

THE NEXT MORNING everyone in Brussels woke to a mood of expectancy. Conversations were sprinkled with the names of Wellington, Blucher, Cochrane, Canning, Uxbridge, Napoleon, Fitzroy, General Alava. There was not one family of the *ton* in Brussels that did not have an officer involved in the battle. Not one who did not fear the outcome of the next few days. But all were determined to mask their fears as far as possible.

On the battlefield nerves were also taut with waiting. Why didn't the French attack? Why was it after eleven before the movement came? Was there another attack occurring somewhere else? Was this a feint? Already the word was out that some of the Prussians had been routed the day before, and everyone wondered if it would happen to them.

As the battle began in earnest, so did the fears of the inhabitants of Brussels. Most maintained that of course it was the French who would be routed, and the distant sound of guns was to be desired as evidence that our men were fighting bravely. But when some of the people who had gone toward the field to see what was going on returned at highest speed talking of a rout, panic took flame. Everyone returning from the road toward Quatre-Bras had a story of almost being run down by cavalry headed away from battle.

In no time desperate gentlemen were trying to obtain horses and carriages to remove their families to the safety of Antwerp. Freddy Leverton made sure the grooms were armed to stand guard over the horses that belonged to himself, the Milfords, and to John Witton. "For," as Freddy said quietly to his friend Witton, "Jason may have need of them all before the fighting is through."

By evening the crowds were divided between the ramparts, where people stood trying to get a glimpse of what was happening, and Lady Charlotte Greville's house, which had become a source of news from Wellington and others. It was there one first heard that the Scottish regiments had borne the worst of it thus far. And while there was regret for their losses, there was also relief that the officers whose families remained in Brussels were therefore relatively safer. The news also came that Wellington had almost been captured but escaped. John and Freddy brought back the news to Lydia and Eleanor that while Jason was thus far all right, Brunswick, a gentleman they could not help but have met, was dead.

Eventually people tried to sleep and some perhaps succeeded, however uneasily.

It was around ten the next morning that another retreat began, an official one ordered by Wellington. This too caused concern among the people of Brussels and would have done more harm had the populace not had the newly arrived wounded to occupy their thoughts more urgently. Some came in carts, others across the saddles of their fellow soldiers' horses, through roads cleared at times by the cursing of officers and the use of the flat side of a sword.

It was as Eleanor and Lydia had predicted. Every available pair of hands was needed to tend to the wounded and comfort the dying. Nowhere, it seemed, was there enough water, enough bandages, enough doctors. It was left to the citizenry to find beds in their homes for as many soldiers as possible, to bind up as many wounds as possible, to hear the last words of those for whom it was already too late.

Witton, Leverton, Eleanor, and Lydia joined the effort to help and soon became separated. The men were needed to carry wounded into houses that had been opened to welcome them, Freddy joking with the wounded as he did so. The two ladies worked in opposite directions to do what they could. A soldier's wife, Lydia ordered up a preparation of egg yolks, oil of roses, and turpentine to put on gunshot wounds, and she and Eleanor each carried a bowl as they worked. One of the more phlegmatic housemaids ran back and forth procuring more of the substance as it was needed.

Eleanor had hesitated, asking, "Wouldn't it be better for the surgeons to cauterize the wound with boiling oil?"

Lydia directed a level look at her young friend. "I suppose there are still surgeons backward enough to do such a thing. But Jason has told me the shock of such treatment often kills as many men as the wound itself. This, he has assured me, is far better, and he has seen enough of such things to know."

Eleanor nodded then and said, "Of course. I'll do as you say."

And then there was no further time for conversation.

Hours later, when there was nothing more she could do and her clothes were already plastered to her skin from the rain that had begun to fall, Freddy Leverton found Eleanor leaning against the railing in front of a house, unsure of exactly where she was or how far she had wandered from the Milford house.

Without a word Leverton put an arm around her waist and began to lead her down the street. His face was as lined and grim now as Eleanor's own, and the eyes haunted with what he, too, had seen. "Lydia?" she managed to ask.

"John is looking for her," Freddy said curtly.

Eleanor nodded, grateful for his strength. In just a few minutes they were home. "So many men in so short a distance," she murmured in wonder. "I thought I had gone at least a mile from here."

Leverton paused on the front steps in the rain, a ghost of a smile once more upon his face. "You are a most remarkable young woman," he said, and then, bending closer, he kissed her with an intensity that took them both unawares.

Eleanor clung to Leverton, and when he finally lifted his lips from hers, she said, with a voice that shook, "I am, at any rate, a most bedraggled one."

At once Freddy grinned, albeit shakily, and said, "Forgive me. You must want nothing so much as a warm bath and a warm meal, and here I am behaving toward you as though . . . as though we were walking in the park instead of finding ourselves in the midst of war."

Eleanor smiled warmly up at him, oblivious to the rain, and a mischievous smile lit her face as she retorted, "And do you commonly kiss girls on walks through parks?"

Leverton colored and with unaccustomed confusion said, "Forgive me. I had not meant to go beyond the line. But you were so beautiful just then."

"Oh, yes, of course. In all my dirt and mud I must have looked wonderful," Eleanor retorted dryly.

"You did," he assured her with another shaky laugh, "however little you may believe it. But come, I'll take you inside. I know you are wishing me at Jericho with my talking."

"Gammon!" Eleanor said, a twinkle warring with the fatigue in her own eyes. "As though compliments were ever unacceptable to a woman. But I am tired. Though not, I fear, as tired as the men fighting. Oh, Freddy, if there are this many soldiers who have managed to reach town, wounded as they are, how many more must there be still on the road or dying on the battlefields too weak to move or be moved?"

Leverton shook his head, not trusting himself to speak. His own thoughts took up the silent questions. How many more men would die or lose their limbs or eyes or minds before this horror was over? And where, in God's name, was Jason?

That was Lydia's question when she arrived, moments later, with Witton. "Has there been word from or about Jason?" she asked, her face white with the same exhaustion and horror the others felt.

Freddy shook his head. "No one knows. Already there have been reports of men dead whom we know to be alive and men alive we know to be dead. I cannot help but think it better we have heard nothing rather than rely on such untrust-worthy reports."

Lydia swallowed deeply and nodded. To Eleanor she said, "You must be as wet and tired as I am. Let us go upstairs and change. And hope that in spite of all this our cook has contrived some sort of repast, though I shall not blame her if she has not."

At this Freddy could not help but grin. "True," he said. "You kept her busy preparing your magic potion. If we starve tonight it shall be all your fault!"

Lydia paused, her hand on the stair railing, and the bleakness once more swept over her face. "Oh, Freddy!" she all but cried. "What of the men on the field, mired in the rain and mud? In this con-fusion how will they eat? How will they cook? We can so easily call for a pot of hot tea or bowl of soup, but what of them? How can they warm themselves in this storm."

It was left to John Witton to reply quietly, "They cannot."

The words were cruel but they were quite correct. By morning there would be men dead because they had been wet and cold and unable to get warm. Nature as well as the French conspired against Wellington, though perhaps it is unfair to say so because Napoleon would also lose men to the elements. Only the officers could count on being warm and dry and fed a warm meal that night, and not even all of those.

It was an even more cruel irony that though the sun broke through the next day in some places, other parts of the battlefield were still afflicted with rain. Once more the battle was delayed and some joked that the French were waiting for the ground to dry before they set forth to fight.

Jason Milford found a brief hour, shortly before dawn, to stop at home and reassure his wife that he was still alive. His forehead, to be sure, carried a surface wound, but he shrugged it off as a mere scratch, nothing compared to what so many had suffered. Then he was gone back to the field knowing that if the worst occurred, he at least had had the chance to say good-bye to Lydia.

Leverton was also awake at that hour, and just before Jason left, the two men had a word in private. The colonel was firm in his belief that Wellington would prevail, but he was not a fool and left a few last instructions should Napoleon break through the lines and head for Brussels. Then, with a warm clasp of hands the two men parted and Milford rode away, taking his best spare horses with him.

By the end of the day, victory would lie with Wellington, but so would the burden of death. Death of his soldiers, death of his officers, death of his friends. Too many would have lost their lives on both sides and too many more would carry scars for the rest of their lives.

Word reached Lydia Milford and Frederick Leverton around dusk that Jason had been wounded. Freddy immediately called for a carriage to take him to the field, but before it could be brought around, Colonel Milford arrived in a cart. He was not conscious and the two men who carried him in told Lydia, "Doctor Hume said we was to bring him here straightaway. Said he would come by when he could and you wasn't to worry, it ain't as bad as it looks. Probably."

With those words they laid Jason on the bed to which Freddy directed them. Lydia meanwhile sent a maid for extra pillows and another blanket. 'What are we to do for him?" she asked the men.

"Dunno," one replied.

"Keep him quiet, the doctor said," replied the other. "That an' watch his fever." Then, after a brief pause he added, "All that blood, ma'am, it ain't his. Leastways not most of it. He brought young Gordon in what lost a leg. Doctor Hume said he thinks it's his head. Gashed a second time he was. But don't you fret. Least he'll live, which is more than can be said for a lot of 'em."

With those encouraging words the men left to deliver other patients to families waiting to care for them. And the household turned its attention to Jason, who seemed not even to know where he was in the rare moments he was conscious.

It was in the midst of all this confusion that the message arrived for Eleanor from the Comte de Beauvais. Her immediate reaction was to refuse to open it, but for the moment there was nothing she could do to help and curiosity got the better of her. Seeking her room so that no one could see and ask her whom it was from, Eleanor sat on her bed and opened the note Beauvais had sealed with his family crest.

My dear Nora,

Fortune is fickle and I find I cannot depend upon Wellington to achieve victory in time to allow me to reclaim my rightful inheritance and meet certain pressing debts. I do not ask you for funds. I merely wish you to understand why I may be pressed to sell certain letters in my care, distasteful as such a step must be to me.

I am sure you will understand.
Your respectful servant,
Jean-Pierre, Comte de Beauvais

Eleanor was under no illusion as to the purpose of this note. She remembered too well just how many letters she had written and the impassioned words she had poured out on paper. Jean-Pierre had sworn to burn them as soon as they were read, and she had been naïve enough to believe him. But now, after the wager he had made concerning the imaginary elopement, she had no doubt that the truth was that he had kept them to use against her if he wished.

In the warmth of her room Eleanor shivered. Who should she go to? Lydia? She could not when Colonel Milford lay so ill and needed all his wife's attention. Leverton? As she thought his name, Eleanor felt a blush color her face a deep red. No, she could not go to him. He was someone she had come to care for far too much. She could not bear to have him see the proof of her folly. And because Leverton was his best friend, Eleanor could not go to John Witton either.

Abruptly Eleanor rose and began to pace about her room. She must see Beauvais, must persuade him to give her the letters. But how? When?

The when was easily answered. Now. There could be no other time so perfect. Confusion was everywhere in Brussels tonight and no one would remark upon her coming or going. For once propriety would be less upon the minds of the populace than simple concern for the men fighting and fears as to who was winning. As for how, well, Jean-Pierre had been thoughtful enough to include directions to his lodgings at the bottom of his letter.

Coming to a decision, Eleanor donned a hooded cloak, took her pin money that remained and all of her jewelry but the pearls, and put them in her reticule. It was not as much as she would have liked, but it was all that she had. Then, with care and a silent apology to her kind hostess, Eleanor slipped out of the house.

13

THE COMTE DE Beauvais had rented rooms on a quiet back street, but like all the other streets in Brussels that night, it was not quiet. Eleanor passed other women alone, many headed for the chemist for medical needs, and she felt another qualm of guilt that her errand was scarcely so noble. Grimly she pressed on until she was rapping at the door of Jean-Pierre's lodgings.

"Ah, Mademoiselle Redmond. Please to come in," he said opening the door.

"You are not surprised to see me?" Eleanor asked coolly.

He spread his hands after closing the door behind her. "But how shall I be surprised?" he asked. "I already know you to be a young lady of resolution and courage, even if that is a secret known only to you and to me." He paused, then added with a charming smile, "I admire your quickness of mind, *ma chère*. To have persuaded Madame Milford to take you with her when you discovered yourself alone on the ship was very intelligent. No doubt you contrived to appear very innocent and forlorn. I wonder what tale you told her?"

Uneasily Eleanor shifted her weight. She could almost have believed the count spoke for the benefit of someone in the other room and she would not have been surprised if he indeed had stooped that low. Aloud she merely replied in the same cool voice as before, "I have nothing to say to you about your absurd wager."

"Ah, yes, you are here about the letters," Beauvais said easily. "I wonder what your charming hostess would say if she were to read them, eh? So indiscreet, so impetuous."

Eleanor turned away from him and stared into the unlit fireplace. With a voice that was strained she said, "I wrote out of what I believed to be love."

Beauvais grinned. "True," he conceded amiably. "And your letters I know to be innocent. But I wonder if your so-charming hostess will believe it? Particularly if I show a page here, a page there, and hint that there is much more said. Will your so charming hostess believe me, I wonder, or you?"

"Stop calling her that!" Eleanor all but shouted as she rounded on the count. "Her name is Lydia Milford and her husband is lying wounded right now! How can you talk of distressing her at a time like this?"

"Very well." Beauvais smiled and shrugged. "I am agreeable. I understand perfectly. In fact, when I think of it, I realize it would be better not to speak to the lady herself."

"Then whom do you mean to speak to?" Eleanor asked warily.

Beauvais spread his hands. "Why, her brother, of course. I believe him to have such an interest in you that even he will wish to see what it is you have written. I wonder if he will still be your devoted admirer after that. As I say, a page here, a page there, a hint of much more." Beauvais shrugged.

Eleanor turned very pale and he went on, "But, of course, even if I succeed in planting these suspicions in Monsieur Leverton's mind, these letters may not change his interest, merely its direction. And perhaps you would enjoy to be set up in a house of your own with such a handsome protector."

Before she could stop herself, Eleanor grabbed the nearest object and hurled it at the count. He ducked, laughing, and it shattered against the far wall. Beauvais tutted her and then said, "*Non, mais non*. You must not kill me yet or you will not be able to find your letters."

"What do you want for them? Money?" Eleanor demanded, shaking.

Again the count spread his hands. "But naturally. How much can you give me?"

It was, of course, not enough. That did not stop Beauvais from taking it. Instead, he told her, icily, "You have bought yourself four days, *ma chère*. If, by then, you do not have five hundred pounds to give me, I shall go straight to Monsieur Leverton with the letters. And if he does not wish to buy them, then all of Brussels shall enjoy the joke at your expense. For it is amusing to see the words of a young lady in love."

"You are a beast!" Eleanor flung at him. "There is no way I can raise that sum of money in four days."

He bowed. "You will try. Four days," he repeated, holding the door open for her.

Beauvais knew, of course, that she would not

have the money by then, but such a short deadline would cause her to act as quickly as possible and he fully expected to have the sum in hand within the week.

With a snap Eleanor pulled the hood of her cloak over her head to shadow her face, and brushed past Beauvais. With tears in her eyes, she made her way back to the house Colonel Milford had hired.

By the time she reached it, she was more composed again and her face was dry. Four days! Time perhaps for an urgent message to be carried to London and back with funds from her parents. Surely her father would not refuse to forward her the money? There was no need for panic yet, no need to fear that Lydia or her brother would ever see those letters.

So great was her relief and so intent was Eleanor on these thoughts that she did not see Frederick Leverton waiting for her in the entrance hall until his icy voice caught her up short. "Where have you been?" he thundered, the anxiety evident in his face.

Startled, Eleanor looked at him with frightened eyes. "I-I had to go out," she stammered.

"Out?" Leverton asked incredulously. "On a night like this? Why? Where could you need to go?"

"Where?" Eleanor repeated blankly. Frederick continued to regard her with burning eyes and finally Eleanor looked away.

Leverton, however, was not satisfied. He seized her by the shoulders and demanded, "Why didn't you take one of us with you? John or myself? And what was so urgent that it couldn't not wait until morning?"

Helplessly Eleanor shook her head, trying to

pull free, still unable to meet his eyes. "I had to go," was all she could say.

Leverton would not release her, however, and his grip only tightened as he said looking down at her, "Indeed?"

In spite of herself, Eleanor placed her hands against his chest as she asked, her eyes anxiously searching his, "Has something happened?"

Concern gave way to anger and abruptly Leverton pushed Eleanor away from him and began to pace about the foyer as he said, incredulously, "My sister's husband is lying ill and wounded upstairs and you ask if anything has happened?"

With an effort Lydia pulled herself together and retorted, "I know that. I meant since I left."

"No. Except that I discovered you chose a time like this to go out. In secret," Leverton replied implacably. "As though my sister has not enough to worry her as it is."

"I chose precisely this time because I did not wish her to know and worry," Eleanor countered, pleading. His eyes were once more turned on her, piercing in their intensity, and with a touch of desperation in her voice, Eleanor said, "I know you will excuse me. I must go upstairs and see if there is any way I can help Lydia."

Leverton started to speak, then changed his mind and let her go. His face was grim, he then went into the library, where he found John Witton drinking a glass of port. "Is she back?" Witton asked quietly.

Leverton nodded. "And she refused to say where she had gone."

Witton came over to his friend and handed Leverton a glass of port but forbore to question him further. Instead, he clapped his friend on the shoulder, then turned away and sat in a chair to wait until Freddy chose to speak.

After several long minutes he did. Turning an agonized face to Witton, Leverton said, "Where could she have gone, John? And why alone? To meet some man? Or for some reason we can't even begin to guess? Is she in trouble or have I been mistaken and her character is hopelessly weak? I don't know which thought distresses me more, John."

"After yesterday—" Witton began.

Freddy cut him short. "Yes, yes, after yesterday I thought her wonderful. And if it were not for Maria, I should think my suspicions impossible. But you recall how she was. At once appearing the heroine and at the same time playing the part of a private harlot. John, what am I to think?"

He fell silent, as did Witton, who had no answer to his friend's question. But after several moments Leverton spoke again. "Will you speak to Miss Redmond?" he asked, quietly this time. "Perhaps she will tell you what she will not tell me." Slowly Witton nodded and Leverton went on, "I cannot shake the fear that something is wrong." Then, after a moment he added, "Do you know, John, I had forgotten how painful love can be."

Upstairs, Lydia Milford was saying almost precisely the same thing to Eleanor. Both ladies stood looking down at the restless figure of Colonel Milford. In a voice that was not altogether steady, Lydia went on, "I think that if Jason does not live I shall not be able to bear it. He has become so much a part of my life, you see, so much a part of my being."

Eleanor placed a comforting arm around the

older woman's shoulders. "They said he was not in danger of dying," Eleanor answered quietly. "Not with our nursing. Why don't you go to bed and rest? I'll stay with him."

Lydia shook her head. "How can I leave him?"

Eleanor smiled wryly. "You will surely collapse by morning if you do not rest now. Recollect that I know you have not slept at all these past two nights for fear of what might happen to your husband."

"You are right, of course," Lydia said, smiling painfully at her young guest. "It is just so hard to leave him."

"I promise I'll get you at once if there is the slightest cause for alarm. Or if he should awaken," Eleanor assured her. "Now please go and rest"

Lydia Milford did as she was bid.

In the morning Lydia's first thought was to go to Jason. Some hours later she made herself go downstairs to speak to her brother. She found him again in the library, still in a grim mood.

"How is Jason?" Leverton promptly asked when Lydia entered the room.

She shook her head. "I cannot say. Nora is with him now. But so far he has not come to himself."

As they stood there, a knock sounded at the door and a moment later the Duke of Wellington was shown into the library. "How is Milford?" he asked curtly.

It was impossible to be offended when everyone could see that the lines of the duke's dismay and fatigue were etched onto his face.

Lydia stepped forward. "Will you take a glass of wine?" she asked.

He shook his head. "I've too many houses to

visit today, too many of my men to see." Wellington paused, then added quietly, "We've won, but at a cost too painful to imagine. Thank God I will not lose Milford as well, though I've no doubt it will be some time before he is fit for duty. Doctor Hume has already warned me of that. Can I see him?"

"Of course," Lydia said, gathering her skirts in one hand and turning toward the door. "Please come this way. Though I fear he may not know you. He has been more unconscious than conscious since he was brought here, and were it not for Doctor Hume's assurances otherwise, I should fear for Jason even more than I already do."

Wellington nodded and followed in exhausted silence up the stairs. Lydia rapped softly on the door of Jason's room, then opened it. Eleanor still sat beside the bed mopping his brow while the colonel tossed feverishly, muttering about dispatches and divisions and cavalry and guns. Wellington watched for a long moment but did not, as Lydia half-expected, turn away. Instead, he stepped to the bed and said firmly, "We've won, Milford. Boney's on the run. Get well, for I shall soon need you to help me track him down."

Though no one had believed Jason aware of anything about him, the duke's voice seemed to reassure him and he stopped thrashing. He even murmured something that might have been an assent.

Wellington nodded. "He'll do," he said to Lydia with grim satisfaction. "I've seen enough death these past three days to know it well, and I do not see death in your husband's face. Nor have his wits deserted him, however feverish he may now be." He paused, then added, "I cannot tell you how many men I have see in just Jason's state. If one were to describe the fever and such, it would all sound just the same, only the particular wounds differ. And most come through right as rain, so you are not to worry, my dear."

Then the Duke of Wellington left the room after assuring Mrs. Milford that she need not show him the way out. When he was gone, Lydia stood for a long moment staring at her husband. Then, as Wellington had done, she spoke to him in a clear, firm voice. "Nora and I shall take excellent care of you, Jason. There is no need to fret."

Once again the words spoken to the colonel seemed to calm him, and with a nod of satisfaction Eleanor yielded her place to Lydia and also turned and left the room. Lydia sat down and quietly began to sponge the colonel's forehead once again.

14

Eleanor went from the sickroom to the dining room. She had had but a few hours of sleep and had not stopped for breakfast before taking over from Lydia again. With relief she noted that the cook had managed to prepare a few dishes that were still warm on the sideboard. She had just sat down and poured herself tea when she heard footsteps behind her. She turned with a start to see Frederick Leverton standing in the doorway. "G-good morning," she stammered.

Carelessly Leverton entered the room and sat down opposite her, his hungry eyes seeming to devour her. "Is it?" he said evenly. "I wonder you have any appetite . . . after last night."

Eleanor colored even as she pretended to misunderstand. "Why, Colonel Milford is doing as well as can be expected. The Duke of Wellington himself assured us of that."

Leverton placed a restraining hand over hers. "That is not what I meant," he said gently, "and you very well know it."

Her appetite suddenly gone, Eleanor made no

effort to eat. Instead, she trembled as she tried fruitlessly to pull her hand free. "What happened last night," she stammered, "is that I went out as I absolutely needed to do. I make no apologies for where I went or what I did."

Leverton's eyes met hers steadily. "Did you go to visit the Comte de Beauvais?" he demanded huskily. His grip moved from her hand to her wrist and tightened.

For a moment Eleanor wanted to say yes, to tell Leverton what had happened, but the thought of him knowing how foolish she had been, seeing the letters she had written, was impossible. And so Eleanor shook her head, then lowered it. "It is not your concern where I went or what I did," she said in a muffled voice, avoiding his eyes.

Leverton rose to his feet, pulling Eleanor with him. Although he was across the table from her, he seemed intolerably close. "Did you go to see Beauvais?" he demanded inexorably.

"No!" Eleanor lied in desperation.

Leverton did not let go, but his tone became milder and his posture more at rest as he said, "What is it, then? And why will you not tell me where you went?"

Not trusting herself to speak, Eleanor merely shook her head.

In the end Leverton released her. They still stood across the table from each other and Eleanor still avoided his eyes as he said, almost impersonally, "Very well. If that is how you wish it. Good day, Miss Redmond."

And he left the dining room, at which point Eleanor found herself weeping silently, grateful that household custom did not dictate a servant to hand out the dishes at breakfast time.

She was still crying when John Witton came into

the room. Observing her hasty attempts to wipe her face, he did not retreat as another gentleman would have done. Instead, he came forward and said mildly, "Freddy appears greatly distressed because you will not talk with him. And you appear great distressed as well. No doubt you are wishing me at Jericho, but it is just possible, you know, that I might be able to help. I am remarkably discreet and need not even tell Freddy what is amiss, if that is your wish."

At any other time Eleanor would have spurned Witton's offer of help outright. It would be as scandalous, as improper for him to see the letters she had written as for any other member of the *ton*. But right now Eleanor felt badly in need of someone to confide in. She started to speak, then sanity reasserted itself and she said, "I believe I shall come about in a few days. But you could post a letter to England for me this morning. To my parents. It is most urgent that I have an answer in four days."

Witton regarded her levelly. "I think it most unlikely you will have a reply in that short a time. Is the matter a serious one?"

Eleanor made herself laugh. "Why, yes, it seems I have run all through my pin money far too quickly and find myself in need of funds."

John Witton did not at once reply. Under his steady gaze Eleanor fidgeted nervously. At last he said, "Of course I shall be delighted to post your letter for you. In fact, I shall try to arrange for it to go straightaway. And should you, er, discover later that there is anything else you wish to confide in me, or any errand you wish me to undertake, please be assured I shall be delighted to be of service."

Then, with a polite bow he was gone. After a

moment Eleanor gave up trying to eat. Instead, she went upstairs and penned a letter home asking for the five hundred pounds.

As soon as the letter was done, she sought out John Witton, ignoring Leverton, who was with him. But Freddy would not have it. Rising to his feet, he held out an imperious hand for her letter.

At Eleanor's startled look he said, a trifle curtly, "It is all right, Miss Redmond. I know about the letter to your parents. John has told me that it must go to England as quickly as possible, and I know someone who is leaving at once. He will see that your parents receive it faster than any other way it could go."

Eleanor hesitated only a moment. Then she handed the letter to Leverton and said quietly, "Thank you." She hastily turned to go, but Leverton's voice stopped her.

"Miss Redmond!" he said. When she turned and looked inquiringly at him, Freddy went on, more gently this time, "I understand you were up most of the night nursing my brother-in-law. I thank you for that, as I am sure Lydia does."

Eleanor quirked a brief smile at Leverton. "It is little enough for me to do," she said. "And one of the few things at which I have had practice. After all, it was I who nursed my brothers and sister through the measles when my mother was laid down on her bed as well."

"You have unexpected talents, it seems," Witton observed gravely.

In a voice that seemed filled with constraint Leverton said, "A great many talents." Then he turned on his heel and was gone from the room, calling over his shoulder to them, "I shall attend to this letter at once."

* * *

Over the next two days Eleanor's court again began to collect around her. Those admirers, at any rate, who had not fallen at Waterloo. In addition, there were many callers who came to see how Jason was.

One morning Dr. Hume called to examine the colonel. Jason was conscious again and most evidently had his wits about him. Dr. Hume pronounced himself satisfied with Milford's progress. Lydia and Eleanor continued to share the nursing, and the colonel steadily, if slowly, regained his health. Wellington called once more to be certain his aide was on the road to recovery and admonished him to rejoin his staff as soon as he was able.

As the days passed, each brought new horrors. Piles of dead horses from the battlefield had to be dragged into piles and burned. Human corpses were buried or burned as well. As far away as the battlefield was, there were many who swore they could smell the stench, and anyone who ventured in that direction returned with a tale of their horses screaming in protest at the odors.

Leverton and Witton went out, more than once, to see if they could help. There were families searching for loved ones among the wounded and newly made widows who needed aid in arranging passage home to England. Freddy ran errands for Wellington, who was desperately short on staff.

Eleanor and Leverton, when he was home, settled into an uneasy truce. Though there was a sense of constraint in his manner, he did not pinch at her as he had before. More and more Eleanor found herself turning to him to talk of how she felt, and more and more she felt the comfort of his quiet good sense. To be sure, the sunny disposition that had cloaked Leverton when Eleanor first knew him was gone, but then, there were few who managed to laugh easily in times such as these. Particularly as day after day brought the news of a new death from among the wounded.

Sir William de Lancey was one of the cases **that** drew the greatest sympathy. Newly married, he had been talking with Wellington on the battlefield when struck and with the devoted nursing of his bride he would, in the end, last nine days before he, too, died.

Nor did the departure for France of Wellington on June 20 serve to raise any spirits. Rather, it made more sure the finality of the battle and the death of those who had fallen. Which was, everyone admitted, an absurd thing to feel but nevertheless undeniably true.

For Eleanor the time seemed to pass quickly as she waited for the reply to the letter she had sent her parents. It was the one thing she could not talk about with Leverton, though many times she felt herself on the verge of doing so. All too soon the day arrived that Beauvais had set for her answer but the letter did not.

Feeling somewhat lost Eleanor went downstairs in search of Lydia. She was nowhere to be found. Neither was Leverton. But John Witton was in the entryway with his bags. "Oh, are you going?" she asked blankly.

Seeing her distress, Witton spoke to the footman, then led Eleanor into the library. "I am returning to my hotel," he said gravely. "Colonel Milford is recovering well and there is no longer any danger in Brussels from Bonaparte." He paused and Eleanor nodded. "I collect there was no letter for you from your family and that has distressed you. Can I help?"

She shook her head. Then, in a low voice she said, "My difficulty is rather plebeian, I am afraid. Mr. Witton, would you be able to lend me money?"

"How much?" Witton asked. "I collect you have somehow acquired a small gambling debt or some such thing."

"Five hundred pounds," Eleanor replied quietly.

It was far in excess of anything Witton had been contemplating. He blinked, then placed his hands on the back of a chair as he replied, "I am afraid, Miss Redmond, that even if I wished to give you the funds, I would find that too large a sum to lend you without knowing what it is for. May I ask how you managed to contract such a large debt these past weeks? I collect it is a debt? Or is it something else?" Witton asked, his voice turning harsh.

Unable to meet his eyes, Eleanor turned away as she said, "It is of no consequence. I-I shall come about, I daresay."

Moving closer to the girl, Witton said gently, "Will you confide in me? Or, better yet, in Leverton. Between us we might be able to help."

Eleanor shook her head. "I think not," she managed to say. Then, brushing past him, she added hurriedly, "You must excuse me. I've just remembered an errand I was supposed to do for Mrs. Milford."

Witton watched her go, then went back to the foyer, where he assured himself that the footman had put his bags in the waiting hack. After he was settled in at his hotel, he certainly meant to go in search of Freddy.

Miss Redmond, meanwhile, went in search of

Beauvais. This time, however, she was not venturing there after dark on a night when everyone's thoughts were preoccupied with battle. Instead, there were a good many censuring eyes to note that she entered a house given over to lodgings for young men. To make matters even more vexing, Eleanor was informed by the landlady that the French gentleman had gone out and she had no idea when he would return.

"Perhaps I might wait in his rooms?" Eleanor asked timidly, conscious of her visible position in the doorway.

"Certainly not!" the good lady replied, shocked. "This is a respectable house. And I must say I would not have taken you for that sort of girl."

"I am not," Eleanor retorted quickly. "I am his —his niece. But I understand your position perfectly. If I might just leave a note for him? Have you paper and ink?"

Grudgingly the woman stood aside as she said, "Very well. Can't have you standing on the doorstep for everyone to see. Come into my parlor and I'll give you what you need to write the note for your uncle. Powerful lot of nieces and cousins that man has," she added darkly, "all of them female and pretty. And all of them in a desperate hurry to see him."

These words penetrated Eleanor's agitated state and she blinked. "Lots of nieces? And cousins?" she repeated musingly. "And all of them desperate?"

The woman peered at Eleanor. "That's what I said, isn't it? Are you touched or something?"

That made Eleanor laugh bitterly. "Only by naïveté," she said. Then more briskly she added, "The paper and ink?"

"If you didn't ask so many questions, you'd have had them by now," the woman retorted crossly, and went to the sideboard, where she found what Eleanor needed.

Then the landlady stood over Miss Redmond as she composed her note. Eleanor and the woman had been conversing in French, which led her to hope that the woman did not understand English. A forlorn hope, she discovered, as the woman said when Eleanor was done, "You won't sway him with that, my dear. A hard man when it comes to money is the count, as I've good reason to know. Nor one with any sort of heart at all. More'n one girl has come away from his door crying and with an emptier purse than when she started."

Eleanor hesitated only a moment, then she stood up and faced the landlady squarely. "You have been very frank with me," she said, "and I thank you for that. In turn, I shall be frank with you. I was naïve enough to write letters to the Comte de Beauvais, love letters, and now he is trying to force me to pay a great sum of money for them. Would you agree to let me into his rooms, or better still, come with me and watch while I search for my letters? I swear that is all I will remove." She paused and added with a grim expression upon her face, "Though I admit I shall be tempted to return any others I find to their rightful owners."

The landlady did not hesitate. "I shall," she said. "For I cannot hold with gentlemen treating you young ladies this way. Come along and I'll help you search."

If Eleanor suspected the landlady had her own additional reasons for helping, she did not say so.

It was enough to know her own ordeal might soon be at an end. That hope, however, was dashed the moment the landlady opened the door to the count's rooms.

"It's empty!" the woman exclaimed in astonishment. "He's gone and left and owes me for a week's rent into the bargain!"

Shaken, Eleanor held on to the doorjamb to support herself. Numbly she heard herself say, "Yes, he's gone. With my letters and all the others as well. Now what am I to do?"

Slowly she walked into the room and looked around. "What could have made him go?" she wondered aloud. "Before he even heard my answer—that I didn't have the money. It doesn't seem like the wretch to leave when there was the least chance he could yet obtain some funds here. And where is he?"

"That I can tell you," the landlady said grimly as she came up behind Eleanor. "He told me more than once these past few days that when he left my lodgings he was going straight to France and demand his rightful inheritance."

Startled, Eleanor looked at the woman. "Isn't that a trifle premature?" she asked. "Wellington has won the battle, not the war."

"Not by what the Comte de Beauvais says," the woman replied. "He says it's only a matter of weeks before the king is back on the throne again. And then he'll have his estate. Meanwhile, he means to spy out the land and see what he's up against."

"Yes, that sounds like Jean-Pierre," Eleanor said slowly. "Just as it is like him to have carried the letters with him, though I don't mean to leave

130

until I have searched the room. If that is all right with you?'

Again the woman's eyes gleamed as she said, "I'll help!"

15

John Witton found Leverton without too much trouble. He quickly told Freddy what Eleanor had said. After a brief silence Leverton said, a hint of steel in his voice, "Do you know, I think perhaps we should pay a visit to the Comte de Beauvais? Miss Redmond told me he was not the person she went to see the other night, but I think we should make sure for ourselves." Witton nodded and Leverton went on in a conversational tone, "I have already obtained the count's direction. Not that that was difficult to do. It seems he owes a great many people in Brussels money and they were all willing to oblige."

Leverton and Witton rapidly set off for that part of town. They arrived soon after Eleanor had left, and the landlady did not seem surprised to have two more visitors asking after Beauvais. "You're not the first to be wanting to see him, not by a long shot," the woman told them. "Nor the last, I'll vow, to be angry to find him gone."

"Gone?" Freddy asked, startled.

"Aye, bound for France I've no doubt," the

woman replied. "It's what he always said he would do if Wellington won. And now that he's gone, I'm sure of it. I've just come from his room and he's taken everything that was his and more than a little that was mine."

"When did he leave?" Leverton asked anxiously. "And was he alone?"

The woman shrugged. "Sometime today, but I didn't see him go. Was he alone? I cannot say."

"Thank you, you have been most kind," Leverton told her, pressing a coin into the woman's hand.

As they walked away, back to the house Colonel Milford had rented, Witton said quietly, "You seemed anxious to know when Beauvais left. Why care, so long as he is gone?"

"Because, for all her denials, I cannot help but believe Beauvais is somehow involved in Miss Redmond's need for money," Leverton replied grimly.

With a laugh Witton clapped his friend on the shoulder. "Freddy," he said, "surely you cannot think Miss Redmond would be so foolish as to try to run off with the fellow again? For I collect that is what you meant when you asked his landlady if he left alone."

"It was," Leverton agreed, his voice still grim. "And I do not think it likely. But I would not put it past Beauvais to try to kidnap her, and I shall be very ill at ease if we do not find Miss Redmond at home when we get there."

To that John Witton had no reply.

Eleanor Redmond had no notion how close upon her heels the two men were. Instead, as she paced about her room, she was conscious only of anger at Beauvais. It would be nonsense to pursue him, she told herself, well aware that her disappearance from Brussels so soon after Beauvais' must cause talk. Madness to trade possible ruin for the certainty of it, which her flight would cause. No, difficult as it was, she must stay here and hope that the Comte de Beauvais did not return. Perhaps no one need ever know about the letters. Surely if Jean-Pierre regained his inheritance, he would no longer need to harass her. Meanwhile, Eleanor would also wait for her parents' letter.

Thus, when Leverton and Witton asked for her, Eleanor was able to come downstairs and appear tolerably calm. When asked about her earlier agitation, Eleanor waved a hand and said with a careless laugh, "Oh, that was nonsense. I had thought to buy something special, but after some thought I realize I must not be so outrageous in my extravagance."

The two men eyed each other skeptically but contented themselves with saying they were pleased to hear it. Then Leverton said casually, "By the by, I have heard that the Comte de Beauvais has left Brussels. You must be delighted to hear me say so."

"I am," Eleanor said emphatically. "Indeed, I pray I never set eyes on the man again."

Once more the two men looked at each other. "I cannot help but think a great many people would be in agreement with you," Witton observed dryly. "Except, of course, those to whom he owed money."

Somehow Eleanor managed a small smile. Silence filled the room for several moments and in the end it was Eleanor who broke it. "I must go upstairs," she said, "and see if Lydia needs me. We are both delighted at the excellent progress Colonel Milford is making. The doctor thinks he will be ready to return to duty soon."

"Let us hope that the worst of the fighting is over by then," Witton said quietly, "though I am quite certain that is not Colonel Milford's philosophy."

"On the contrary," Leverton replied. "I have heard Jason say more than once that the sooner the killing is over, the better pleased he will be."

Witton nodded. "You are right. I meant rather to say that Colonel Milford will be distressed that he has not been at Wellington's side through all this. Your sister says that already he begins to think himself a shirker, though the doctor has emphatically told him otherwise."

All three nodded. Everyone in the household had heard *that* discussion between the doctor and the colonel, and it was only Lydia's firmness that had given the doctor the upper hand in the matter. Keeping the colonel quiet another week would not be an easy task, and Eleanor quite frankly did not believe they would succeed. Even Lydia had told her privately that she thought her husband would be on his horse and away before many more days passed.

In his quiet voice Leverton said, "I cannot help but honor Jason for that. Wellington lost a great many men, too many of them his friends. Jason is not wrong in saying the man needs him."

"Lydia has already said that she will not stop Colonel Milford when he feels ready to leave," Eleanor said quietly, "but he is not to know that. Otherwise, he would insist upon leaving today."

The talk between the two men turned to politics

and the current situation in France and speculation as to when Louis XVIII would leave Ghent for Paris or if, in fact, he had already begun the journey. And in the end Eleanor slipped away unseen.

Up in her room Miss Redmond found Lydia Milford's maid waiting for her. With a curtsy the woman said, "Mrs. Milford told me I was to ask you which gown you meant to wear tonight. She said if it was the rose one, I was to repair a rip in the hem."

Startled Eleanor replied, "Yes, I did mean to wear the rose gown and I had forgotten the tear. Here it is, and thank you."

"You're very welcome, I'm sure," the woman replied with another curtsy.

Then Eleanor was alone and she found herself, for the first time since her come-out, thinking of a party as a tiresome chore to be endured rather than enjoyed. Nevertheless, she was young and resolutely she shook off her mood. After all, for the first time in weeks she could be certain she would not see Jean-Pierre or be obliged to endure his barbed remarks. In any event, Colonel Milford had decreed that his wife and her young guest should attend, and neither lady would upset him by refusing.

So it was that at nine o'clock that evening Lydia Milford, her brother Frederick, and their guest Eleanor set off for the quiet farewell ball one of the ladies was giving. Lydia wore a gown of royal blue that set off her fair coloring marvelously, and Eleanor wore the rose. Although she had given Beauvais almost all of her jewelry, Eleanor had held back her set of pearls and it was these she now wore. Colonel Milford, who had asked to see the two ladies in all their finery and fluff, as he called it, pronounced them exquisite and himself jealous not to be going. Then he ordered them on their way, consigning them to Leverton's care.

Freddy was only too happy to oblige.

The house was crowded. Everyone in Brussels who could come, it seemed, was there, whether they had been invited or not. And all of them talking politics. But the difference between this ball and those held before the battle was only too evident. The fine British uniforms that had been such an important part of the festivities before were now absent, their owners busy in France. And among the local soldiers, too many faces were absent. As were many of the ladies, local and otherwise. When one asked why, the answer would usually come, almost in a whisper, "In mourning," or "Tending her wounded husband" or "brother" or "son" or "uncle" or "cousin." Everywhere there was evidence of the toll the battle had taken, and it seemed to Eleanor that not a family had gone untouched. Even the music was not as gay and bright as it had been before the battle, and while those of Eleanor's suitors left in Brussels still clamored to dance with her, she could not help but be aware that the dance floor was the one place in the room not crowded.

It was close upon midnight when Eleanor realized that a number of people were staring at her and that her last partner had seemed surprisingly willing to relinquish her at the end of the song. As she stood at the edge of the dance floor trying to puzzle it out, Eleanor saw Leverton coming toward her. With a silly grin he held out a hand and said, "My dance, I believe, Miss Redmond."

The bright smile upon his face did not reach his eyes, and it was that unexpected grimness that made Eleanor agree with a false smile of her own. As he led her onto the floor, however, she whispered to him, "But I had promised this dance to someone else."

"Young Jimmy?" Leverton hazarded. When Eleanor nodded, he smiled lazily though the words were curt, "Jimmy will not be coming to claim the dance, I assure you."

In spite of her determination, Eleanor's smile faltered. "Why not?" she demanded. "He particularly made me promise him a waltz."

As Leverton's strong arm went around Eleanor's waist, he told her, "Because his mother won't let him." At her startled expression he added, "It seems that certain letters you wrote to the Comte de Beauvais have been circulating this evening in Brussels and have reached this dance. I thought I had best warn you. Not that you would have been left partnerless. Apparently a number of gentlemen are quite eager to see if you could be as warm with them as you were in your letters."

Eleanor, who had gone a deep red, now went utterly pale, and a small sob escaped her.

"Smile," Leverton admonished her sharply. "Laugh as though you had not a care in the world. Give the lie to these letters, at least for now, and later at home we can try to think of what else we can do about them."

With his cool words Eleanor managed somehow to regain her composure. Lightly she laughed, and speaking more loudly so that other dancers could hear, she repeated to Leverton an amusing story someone had told her. He laughed and this time his eyes smiled approval at her as well. Then, all too soon the music stopped and Freddy was leading Eleanor from the dance floor. As he had predicted, she had a number of admirers waiting to dance with her. But they were her older suitors and some she had not seen before. These had a harder look about them and more than one a reputation Lydia had taken great care to warn her about.

As though she had not noticed, however, Eleanor laughed and chose the mildest of these to partner her in the next dance, which was not, she was grateful to see, a waltz.

Somehow Eleanor made it through the rest of the evening. Her carefree appearance as well as the careless way both Lydia Milford and Freddy Leverton shrugged off the infamous letters as another fabrication, indeed forgery, of the Comte de Beauvais went a long way to planting doubt in the minds of those who were there. Still, those carefree smiles dropped away the moment Freddy handed Lydia and Eleanor into the carriage to go home.

"John and I shall try to obtain the letters," Leverton said grimly. "You must go on ahead and we will follow as soon as possible."

"It is a disaster. But no one can believe this for long," Lydia said to Eleanor, trying to reassure her as the carriage lurched forward over the cobblestones. "It is absurd to think you could have written these letters, and when they see your real handwriting, they will know it is only an attempt by the count to get revenge."

Eleanor shrank miserably into her corner. "But it is my handwriting," she replied.

Lydia answered slowly. "I see. Was it because of these letters that you went out the night Jason was wounded? To see Beauvais, I collect?" she asked. "Oh, yes, I heard about that. But, Nora, my dear, I wish you had been able to confide in me, if not in my brother. With a blackguard such as Beauvais the demands would never have stopped, and sooner or later he would have released the letters. To humiliate you if for no other reason."

Lydia's words cut into Eleanor like a whip and she shrank farther against the squabs. "I meant to have them back before I gave him the money," she replied with a touch of spirit.

"And if he had refused? Would you not have paid just to buy yourself time?" Lydia persisted.

Miserably Eleanor nodded. Almost in a whisper she said, "Why does he hate me so very much? Why does he risk his own reputation to destroy mine? All I ever did to him was to imagine myself in love with the fellow, and that was at his own urging."

"And snub him whenever you could, here in Brussels," Lydia quietly replied. She paused and after a moment added, "I cannot understand a man like Beauvais or what drives him to such lengths. I can only see what he does and know he must be stopped. Perhaps you remind him of someone who once hurt him very badly. Or perhaps he simply hates women. There are, I collect, letters written by other young ladies as well, but I will grant you that he seems to hate you most of all."

In a thoughtful voice Lydia added, "Do you know, I seem to recall my mama once taking me to purchase a straw hat made by a woman who might have been the Comte de Beauvais' mother. Many ladies who fled France when the revolution came supported themselves that way. It must have seemed very humiliating to them and perhaps Beauvais has never forgiven us for being more fortunate. Certainly he never speaks of her or how his family supported themselves in England."

Eleanor nodded, feeling even more abashed as Lydia added mildly, "But whatever the reason for his behavior, Nora, you really should have trusted us. We would have helped you, my dear."

16

WHEN THEY REACHED the house, Lydia immediately went upstairs to check on Jason. Eleanor would have gone upstairs as well but Lydia stopped her. "Freddy and John Witton will be here soon with the letters," she said quietly. "I think you will wish to be downstairs when they arrive."

Eleanor nodded. "You are right, of course," she said. "I shall wait for them in the library."

It was a long half-hour that Eleanor waited. Leverton was the first one to join her in the library. Startled, Eleanor looked up at him with eyes that reminded Leverton of a frightened rabbit, and a smile quirked at the corners of his mouth. Hastily he turned away and straightened some papers on his desk. Over his shoulder he asked carelessly, "Why didn't you tell me about the letters?"

Eleanor looked down at her hands. "If you have seen them, or heard what they said," she replied quietly, "then you know that I was foolish enough to write . . . write more warmly than was wise. I didn't want you to read them." She paused, then added, a trifle defiantly, "That is also why I lied to you and said it was not the Comte de Beauvais I had gone to see. It is useless, I suppose, to ask you to believe I was so naïve as to believe him when he said he meant to burn them straightaway. Or that I could buy them back and it would all be over and done with. I must suppose that all of your sister's kind efforts to protect my reputation have, in the end, been for nothing." Briefly Eleanor's voice trembled and she asked, "Will Lydia want me to go when she learns what I wrote in those letters?"

By now Leverton had turned to face Eleanor, and though she did not look at him, he was regarding her with something akin to amused kindness as he started toward her. He was stopped, however, by the sound of a short knock at the door. "Come in," he said loudly.

It was Witton with Lydia at his side.

"How is Colonel Milford?" Eleanor asked hastily.

Lydia smiled briefly. "Much better. And more impatient than ever to join Wellington. I think I have convinced him to wait at least a few more days." She paused, then turned to her brother. "Freddy," she said, "do you have the letters?"

Leverton made an effort to appear grave as he handed them into Lydia's outstretched hand. As she read them, no one spoke and Eleanor shrank farther into her chair, her face pale with the strain of waiting. When Lydia was done, she handed the letters back to her brother. To Eleanor she said, matter-of-factly, "It is always incredible to me to discover just how horribly some men may behave. I collect you wrote these in the first blush of love and he has been cruel enough to spread them about."

"And clever enough to show only a few pages and hint that the others contain far worse," Leverton added, grimness momentarily banishing his smile.

"H-how did you know?" Eleanor asked.

Lydia grimaced. "I am not a green girl in my first Season, but I once was. And over the past few years I have seen a good many blackguards, some of them not above trying to force an heiress into marriage by the most despicable means."

"Yes, but Beauvais doesn't want to marry me," Eleanor protested.

Lydia shuddered. "Thank God for that!" she said. "You are fortunate, though I know it cannot seem so at the moment. And yet I assure you that however society in general may feel, it is my opinion that ruin is far better than being shackled to a man like Beauvais. You are fortunate he only wishes to revenge himself on you by such a shabby trick as this. The question is, how are we to turn this around and reflect upon him?"

"That is done merely by the fact that Beauvais himself set these letters about," Leverton replied with a shrug. "As John and I have taken care to point out to everyone at the ball."

Witton nodded. "I also found out what has happened to the count. An irate husband shot at him and Beauvais decided to leave for France at once. But before he left, he gave these and letters from a few other ladies to friends to circulate. He appears to have been remarkably adroit in getting women to write to him." Witton paused, then added judiciously, "Beauvais is considered bad *ton* just now, but there is also a certain amount of blame being placed upon Miss Redmond. Most people are not as kind as Mrs. Milford. It is the general feeling that young ladies ought not to write such letters to men."

"And is that what you think?" Eleanor demanded hotly, rising to her feet to confront Witton.

He shrugged. "Me? I have no opinion on the subject." He paused, then added, "Other than to say I think it remarkably foolish. Scarcely scandalous, however."

"Thank you, John," Lydia said, placing a comforting arm around Eleanor's shoulders. "Freddy, what do you advise?"

Leverton did not answer at once. Again the smile quirked at the corners of his mouth, much to the exasperation of his sister. At last he said, however, "We cannot deny the letters. To do so is only to make matters worse. Besides, if we did, I should not be surprised to find that one of Beauvais' comrades will swear that he saw her give the letter to the count. Or something of the sort. I think our best course is frankness. And while it will be unpleasant for Miss Redmond, she will come about. Though there may be some who will never forgive her indiscretion."

"How unfair!" Lydia said crossly.

Now Leverton's smile danced about his face as he replied, "And you cannot bear unfairness, can you? But just as you had to learn that heedless actions have consequences, so too must Miss Redmond. John, what do you think?"

Witton sighed heavily. "I confess I see no alternative, though I am less sanguine as to Miss Redmond's reacceptance. Were she less beautiful and had she been less popular this Season, forgiveness would be more readily forthcoming. It is a pity Beauvais is not here to be held to account."

As the other three stood staring at her, Eleanor found herself recalling every heedless thing she had said to her suitors this past Season and every time she had outshone a less attractive or popular girl. "What do I do?" she asked the others flatly. "Return to London?"

Lydia shook her head emphatically. "No! If you do so, if the *ton* sees you run away, they will be after you like a pack of wolves after a lamb. No, you must stand your ground and face them, however difficult that may be."

Witton smiled one of his rare smiles. "Recollect that here you will have us to stand by you, and that will count for more than a little. In London I am sure your family would stand by you as well, but it would be said that they had no choice but to do so."

Feeling very close to tears, Eleanor nodded and murmured something about "kindness."

"Fustian," Lydia retorted roundly. "There is not a one of us here who does not wish to throttle the Comte de Beauvais. What I don't understand is why, if Beauvais had so many women write letters to him and then held them ransom for money, word has not leaked out before now."

"I suspect," Leverton said quietly, "that he simply held on to the letters until now, knowing that someday they might be worth money to him or offer the chance to humiliate someone. But he also must have known that the trick could be tried only once, that after that every lady would be on her guard against him."

"I suppose so," Lydia said with a sigh. "It is a lowering reflection that such a man could succeed so well."

"It is a more lowering reflection to think that

everyone has had some notion the man was a blackguard and yet he was everywhere received," her brother countered.

"Why was he?" Eleanor demanded hotly, asking the same question for the hundredth time.

"Because he was an émigré. Because one felt sorry for him. Because he was handsome in spite of everything," Lydia replied wryly. Then, noting the drawn look upon Nora's face, she said, "Now up to bed with you. Tomorrow you must look your best and be able to appear completely at ease when we go out and about."

"A moment," Leverton said, forestalling her. "I should like to talk to Miss Redmond. Alone."

Lydia looked at her brother in astonishment, but Witton merely raised his eyebrows, then nodded as he rose to his feet. "But it is not the thing," Lydia managed to protest.

"Nevertheless I should like to do so," Freddy said implacably.

Recognizing the steely glint behind her brother's lazy smile, Lydia gave in and allowed Witton to escort her from the room. "Just five minutes, mind!" was her parting shot.

Eleanor and Leverton waited silently until they were gone and the door closed behind them. Then Freddy seated himself on the edge of the desk, his arms crossed against his chest. Eleanor tried to look everywhere but at the smile upon his face. After a few moments Leverton took pity on her distress and came to stand beside her chair. Still she would not look at him. "It is not really so very bad," he said.

Eleanor looked up at Leverton. Taking her chin in his hand, he gently drew her to her feet. "But John Witton said—" she began.

"John Witton is a Friday-faced fellow," Leverton retorted, his eyes twinkling with amusement. "And while I do not doubt that the next few days will be difficult, that you will be chided by all manner of self-righteous persons, I also do not doubt that you will come about. What seems so terrible to you, just now, is really no worse than the silly writings of a girl just out of the schoolroom, which no person of real sense can doubt."

Incensed by these words, Eleanor pulled her chin free and, tilting it up in the air, turned her back upon Leverton. "Indeed?" she demanded frostily, tapping her foot angrily on the floor.

"Indeed," he agreed gently as he turned her back to face him. "Had they been more than that, I should have known it."

"How?" she demanded, her breath starting to come in ragged gasps.

For an answer, though it was not really an answer, Leverton slowly lowered his face to hers and captured her lips easily with his own. The kiss that started out so lightly soon turned deep and searing as the two clung to each other, unaware how tightly they embraced. When at last Leverton let her go, Eleanor felt as though she might faint, so rapidly was her heart beating and so heated did her cheeks feel against his chest where he cradled her. Gently resting his chin upon the top of her head, he said quietly, "Had you been to Beauvais what he wished the world to think, your words would have been far different than they were. And you would not tremble as you do when I kiss you."

Shaken, Eleanor could only nod. She or Freddy might have said more, but it was at that moment that Lydia reentered the room to tell them imperiously, "Freddy! Unhand her this minute! It is time for Nora to go up to bed. And, Freddy, I shall speak to you later."

Meekly he let her go and meekly Eleanor followed Lydia upstairs.

John Witton waited until they were gone, then he quietly closed the door behind them so that the two ladies would not hear what he said to Leverton. "What do you mean to do now, Freddy?" he asked.

Leverton shrugged. "I should like nothing better than to go after Beauvais and call him out. But you know very well I cannot leave my sister alone here. Not when she has Jason on her hands still wounded." He leaned back in a chair and crossed one neatly clad leg over the other, smiling impishly as he added, "I am well aware that even if I could go, fighting Beauvais would accomplish nothing."

"Nothing except to provide more gossip to be linked with Miss Redmond's name," Witton observed disapprovingly.

"What, then, do you suggest?" Leverton asked mildly.

"Let me think upon it," Witton replied calmly. "In the meantime, since we don't know where the fellow is, the question is all but irrelevant."

"Not if we could send someone to find Beauvais," Leverton said triumphantly.

"Yes, but who?" Witton asked.

"Someone Wellington used to gather information, perhaps. Someone accustomed to moving about in France and who knows what is afoot. After all, we know that Beauvais must go to the authorities if he is trying to regain his inheritance," Leverton suggested.

"Unless Beauvais goes straight to Louis the Eighteenth," Witton replied grimly. "And he is still in this country. But otherwise, yes, I suppose it might work. I assume that Wellington did employ such people and that Colonel Milford might know who they are. Do you think your brother-in-law is well enough, however, for us to bother him about this matter?"

Freddy grinned. "If I know Jason, he will be delighted to have something to do and will enjoy thrusting a spoke in Beauvais' plans."

The cause of all this consternation was at that moment mopping his brow at a small inn just inside France. He had thus far eluded the husband who had tried to shoot him with a pistol, as well as the brother who had tried to run him through with a butcher knife. He ought, he supposed, have simply gone to a whorehouse in Brussels, as usual. But how was he to know the lower classes here took their women's virtue so seriously?

Well, at least, he told himself with grim satisfaction, he had left behind something to pay back Miss Redmond for her rude treatment of him in Brussels. And he had made more than a little from the sale of certain other letters to certain other ladies, not all of them young or single, for Beauvais had been hoarding such letters for years. In particular, Lady Deerfield had been most generous when he had returned hers, especially after he had reminded her that it really was his duty to turn them over to Lord Deerfield.

Still, there was no margin for error in the count's plans. He would need some of those funds in dealing with officials in Paris when he got there. And should power change hands again, he must be prepared to deal with that as well. But, Beauvais thought grimly, he would prevail. He would, once more, take his rightful place at court as the Comte de Beauvais and then let laugh who will. He would marry whatever lady he chose and no one would dare humiliate him again. And never would he forgive those Bonapartists on his estates who helped to betray his family to the revolution. In one corner of France the old order would again prevail, upon that he was determined. If he only made it there safely. . . .

With that grim reminder, Beauvais looked quickly around the taproom of the inn again, eyes alert for Bonapartists or angry relatives. When he saw that no one was paying the least attention to him, he once more began to relax. Soon a pleased grin spread slowly over his face, and the innkeeper was kept busy refilling his glass.

17

Monsieur Henri Dubois, as he called himself, was a man well-known to any of the officers on Wellington's staff. In the days before Waterloo he had come and gone as he pleased, and the duke had considered his information invaluable. The fact that no one was ever entirely certain where his true loyalties lay only added spice to the situation.

It was Jason Milford's private opinion that Dubois didn't have any loyalties, except to his own pocket, but that once bought, he stayed bought, which was no small point in his favor. And the man appeared to be clever.

"Look," Milford said to his brother-in-law and to John Witton the next morning as the three men held a private conference around his bed, "Wellington trusted him. And I have never known the duke to be wrong in doing so."

"Besides," Leverton added reasonably, "what could Dubois have to betray? The knowledge that we wish to know the whereabouts of the Comte de

Beauvais? Half the *ton* assumes as much already! What do you think, John?"

Witton smiled grimly. "I think you would prefer to find Beauvais ourself, Freddy, and give the fellow a badly needed thrashing."

Leverton grinned. "So I would. But you needn't fear, I shan't do anything so foolish."

"I am glad to hear it," Jason said, his eyes twinkling. "What do you mean to do if Dubois finds him?"

"Miss Redmond confided in Lydia that Beauvais still holds some of her letters. And that he took all of her jewels, except her pearls, in partial payment for them. Then he left Brussels without even waiting to see if she could produce the rest of the money he demanded," Leverton explained.

"Ah, yes, Lydia did say something about an irate husband chasing Beauvais out of Brussels," Milford said. "So, you mean to recover Miss Redmond's letters and jewels?"

"If I can," Leverton said as he nodded. "Otherwise, she shall always be afraid he will use them against her at some time in the future. Useless to try to tell her that no person of sense will care."

"Particularly when there are so many members of the *ton* who lack sense," Witton added curtly.

"Well, Dubois is the man for you, then," Milford said again. "Discreet as well as clever."

"Where can we find this Dubois? If he is still in Brussels, of course," Freddy said patiently.

Milford named a few places, then added quietly, "If you cannot find him, then I shall rejoin Wellington's staff a few days early. It may be possible to find word of him there."

"I will not have you putting yourself in jeopardy

by returning to duty before you are ready," Leverton told his brother-in-law bluntly. "Lydia would never forgive us and I should never forgive myself if anything happened to you."

Milford merely said, "Well, you and Witton can check Brussels first anyway. Who knows? You may be fortunate enough to find Dubois right here. If not, why, then, we shall see. I think I am in excellent health already."

If the doctor would not go quite that far, he did at any rate, later that day, pronounce himself satisfied with the colonel's progress and finally agreed to allow him out of bed and even out of doors. "Mind now," the doctor said sternly, "you are not to overdo the fresh air or the exertion. But if you feel up to it, you may take a turn or two about the garden."

With a sigh of exasperation Milford retorted, "For heaven's sake, man, it was only a graze to the head and all but healed by now."

The doctor leaned on his medical bag. "All but healed," he repeated sarcastically. "Only a graze to the head. Good God, man, don't you understand you could have died? A blow or injury to the head is one of the things we know least about. I have seen a man take a blow, appear to be fine, and then drop dead without warning, hours or days later. It is your life, of course, to risk as you choose, but I have no desire to tangle with your Duke of Wellington and have to explain to him how a patient of mine who seemed well on the road to recovery suddenly died. Good day, Colonel Milford!" With that, the doctor left, closing the door behind him with a distinct slam.

The colonel turned to his wife, who was regarding him every bit as sternly as the doctor had. "Now, Lydia," Milford began.

"I don't want to hear about it," she said distinctly. "I want to hear that you mean to be as careful as the doctor said you should be, and if you can't say that, I don't want to hear anything else." Lydia stopped and relented a trifle. Moving next to the bed, she sat on it and put her arms around her husband's neck. "I don't mean to scold," she said, resting her head against his shoulder, "it is just that I don't know what I should do if I ever lost you."

Meanwhile, Lady Redmond's letter finally arrived and Eleanor read it with bitter humor.

My dearest Nora,

We were distressed to hear of Colonel Milford's injuries and trust he is recovering well. And we were relieved to hear you were not threatened by the fighting.

As for your requests for funds, we must refuse. You say the need is urgent but will not explain. Well, your father and I are sympathetic to the expenses incurred by a young lady in your position, but we really cannot encourage such extravagance. It is extravagance, we presume, and not some new source of scandal you have become involved in? In any event, the funds already allocated to your account should have been more than sufficient and we refuse to forward such a sum as you have requested. Instead, we are sending you a modest sum more suitable to a girl your age.

Your loving mama,
Lady Redmond

Eleanor carefully folded the letter and put it away. The contents were no surprise, and suddenly it seemed incredible to her that she could have ever believed they might be different. What she needed now was not money but the support of the Milfords and Leverton and Witton. With their help Eleanor weathered the next few days. She had very little choice. What made it at all bearable was that the members of the *ton* began to leave Brussels, a few at a time. Some returned to England, others made plans to follow Wellington to Paris.

"Well, Lydia, do we join the general exodus?" Leverton asked his sister with a grin several days later, one leg casually swung over the arm of his chair.

She stood by the window in the parlor and said, with a smile, "I don't know. Jason has not yet heard from Wellington, Freddy. And until he does, I can make no definite plans. I cannot even be sure he will be sent to Paris and not somewhere else instead."

"Yes, but you are obviously restless," Leverton countered. "Why not tell me what you are thinking?"

Lydia let the corner of the curtain fall as she turned full face to her brother and said, with a sigh, "You know me far too well, Freddy. I am wishing we could go to Paris, for I have never been there and who knows what may happen next to prevent me from going later."

"Then, go," Leverton said promptly, with his boyish smile. "There can be no danger if Louis the Eighteenth goes. And it will do Miss Redmond good to see the city as well."

At that Lydia looked at her brother in surprise.

"Indeed?" she said with raised eyebrows. "I should have thought you would want Nora out of France and away from the Comte de Beauvais." Lydia paused, then added suspiciously, "Has this anything to do with John Witton's visit yesterday? I collect he is already planning to depart for Paris and wishes you to join him, is that it?"

Leverton hesitated. He found he did not wish to tell his sister about Dubois and the arrangements they had made for him to contact them in Paris. Instead, he spread his hands helplessly and said in an injured tone, "You, all of you, call John so sober and staid, but the fellow wants company in exploring the, er, delights of Paris. What else would he do but ask me to come along?"

"You men!" Lydia said in exasperation. "There must not be the slightest tarnish to a woman's reputation, not the slightest hint of scandal. But you may all carry on as scurrilously as you wish with no one to say more than that you are men. It is simply not fair."

Leverton rose and kissed his sister on the cheek. "An old grievance of yours and one I will not dispute," he told his sister with a laugh. A moment later he added lightly, "Do we go? I don't want to abandon you and Miss Redmond here; in fact, I shan't. But I'll tell you frankly that I should like to see Paris too."

Lydia made another sound of exasperation, then said, a twinkle in her own eyes, "Yes, we shall go to Paris, unless Jason expressly forbids it. Indeed, I know he is eager to rejoin Wellington. We need only have word that Jason is well enough to travel and that the duke commands the city. Then you shall tell me how soon we may leave and I'll warrant to have everything packed up in time. But

157

you must close out the house here and handle the travel problems. I don't want any more worries on Jason's shoulders."

"Of course." Leverton paused, then said in a voice that was, for once, serious, "Will Lord and Lady Redmond object, do you think, that we mean to take their daughter to Paris?"

For a moment Lydia's smile turned grim as she replied, "I have heard very little from Lord and Lady Redmond aside from a civil note thanking me for taking Nora into my care. I begin to think that so long as we are willing to undertake her care and protection, Lord and Lady Redmond have not the slightest objection to anything we wish to do. But in any event I have already written to tell them I expect to remove to Paris very soon."

In London, Lord and Lady Redmond were beginning to wonder if they should have given Mrs. Milford such complete charge of their daughter. Lady Redmond held the latest letter from Lydia and spoke with some concern to her husband. "Do you think we should allow it?" she asked.

Lord Redmond looked at his wife with some surprise. "Allow it?" he repeated. "I don't see how we can very well forbid Mrs. Milford to take Nora to Paris. After all, if she wishes to go there, she must take Nora or else abandon her in Brussels, which I scarcely think is what you wish."

"Yes, I know," Lady Redmond replied slowly, as though groping her way, "but I cannot help feeling uneasy at the thought of Nora in France. Particularly coming, as this news does, hard upon the heels of Nora's strange request for money. What *can* she have wanted five hundred pounds for? Because of those letters Lady Crane said Nora is supposed to have written to Beauvais? Could she have been so foolish? And if she was, why didn't she tell us?"

"Perhaps she felt too ashamed to do so," Lord Redmond replied calmly.

"Well, perhaps we ought to go over there and take charge of Nora ourselves," Lady Redmond retorted in patent exasperation.

"But, my dear," Lord Redmond remonstrated, "how can we? There is Amanda to think of, unless you mean we are to take her along as well. And what of the boys? Douglas and Hubert have long since finished the term and arrived home from school. Are they to spend the summer entirely alone?"

Lady Redmond rose and began to pace about the room with some agitation. "You are right, of course. We should have removed back to the country some weeks ago. But I am still concerned about Nora."

"Well, and so am I," Lord Redmond replied, a trifle indignantly, "but she has made her bed and now let her deal with it. I don't see what we can do."

"Perhaps not, but I do," Lady Redmond said with some decision. "If Nora starts out for Paris, then I shall go there as soon as word comes that it is safe to do so, and you shall return home with Amanda and spend some time with the boys. See that they keep out of mischief, that sort of thing."

"My dear wife, that is precisely what I hired their tutor for," Lord Redmond said witheringly.

Lady Redmond waved a hand and said carelessly, "Well, do something with them, anyway, if you think they are in danger of feeling neglected. But if N ora goes to Paris, then I am going to Paris!"

18

Ironically, a message arrived the next morning for Colonel Milford. He was not called directly to rejoin Wellington. Instead, he was to join Louis XVIII's entourage at Cambrai.

"But why?" was Lydia's first question.

"Because," Jason replied patiently, "Wellington does not entirely trust Louis or what he may do, and wants someone there to keep an eye on what he is about. And as I am acquainted with Talleyrand, as well as having been presented to the king, Wellington thought me the ideal choice. There has already been one disastrous incident at Mons, where Talleyrand somehow offended his majesty and the king dismissed Talleyrand from his service. A number of people intervened and Talleyrand has once more joined Louis, but Wellington is understandably concerned. Without Talleyrand it shall be difficult to make Louis palatable to the French people."

"Will the king accept your presence at Cambrai?" Leverton asked. "What excuse will you give for being there?"

Milford nodded. "Wellington has already written to Louis begging his indulgence on my behalf. And given me a letter to present as well. It states that inasmuch as I am still recovering from my injuries, Wellington wishes me to stay somewhat back of the action and in a place with as much protection as possible. The king will know, of course, that it is an excuse, but he will not, I think, refuse."

"What of us?" Leverton asked lazily. "Do we stay here or travel with you?"

The colonel shook his head and with a smile at them said, "No, you come with me. You, Lydia, shall be my devoted wife nursing me through my recovery. Freddy, you are her devoted brother, and Miss Redmond her devoted friend. And I guarantee you shall find it a most interesting experience."

"That I don't doubt," Freddy replied dryly.

Milford hesitated, then added carefully, "I think you may prove very useful to me, Freddy. You could carry messages from me to Wellington and back. If you do not mind."

"Mind?" Leverton said with a laugh. "I think I shall delight in the role."

"Good," Milford said decisively. Then, with a grin, he added, "You are an excellent man to have at hand in spite of your sometimes foppish ways. We leave at once."

"Calumny!" Leverton retorted with a grin of his own.

But Lydia was not to be diverted. "We leave at once?" she asked faintly.

"Well, I must leave by noon," Milford amended. "Wellington wishes me to join the king as soon as possible. And I thought you would want to travel with me. I have already taken care of most of the arrangements. Can you be ready in time? Can Miss Redmond?"

"Of course," Lydia told her husband fondly. "But are you well enough to travel?" Lydia added a trifle anxiously. "The doctor—"

"The doctor does not serve on Wellington's staff," Milford replied grimly. Then, at the sight of her alarmed face, the colonel told his wife, "Come, Lydia, don't fear for me. I assure you I am well enough to travel. But we must go."

After staring at her husband steadily for some moments, Lydia finally nodded, a note of resignation in her voice as she said, "I shall tell Miss Redmond to prepare to leave at once."

"And I," Leverton said with his careless grin, "shall send word to Witton just how privileged we are and that we shall see him in Paris."

Eleanor had no objection to joining Louis XVIII's entourage. Indeed, she was more than a little in awe of the opportunity to, as she put it, take part in the making of history. Lydia had not been able to entirely suppress a smile at that. "The king may not be what you expect," she warned her young guest. "I saw him in London last year and he was not a prepossessing figure. However, he is a Bourbon and will no doubt soon sit on the throne of France once more."

"If the French people will accept him," Freddy interjected. "They may not find it easy to forget that just two days after he wore the Legion of Honor ribbon this past March and pledged to die in defense of France, he fled the Tuileries in his bedroom slippers."

"And that," Colonel Milford said, joining his

wife and the others, "is why Talleyrand's presence is so essential. Of all men he will know how to make Louis palatable or at least how to convince France as well as the allies that the king must sit on the throne again."

"Then he is the man I most wish to see," Lydia said thoughtfully.

"So you shall, *if* we leave now and join the king," her husband said determinedly.

With a laugh the three hurried out to the waiting carriages and began the journey to Cambrai.

Colonel Milford and his party reached Cambrai early in the evening on June 28. Jason was noticeably tired and Lydia tried to persuade him to go straight to his bed, but he shook his head. "I dare not," he told her firmly but with a smile. "That is precisely what Talleyrand is rumored to have done at Mons and it almost cost him his position. And I assure you I am far less important to Louis than Talleyrand."

"But are you well enough to go?" Lydia persisted, noting the pallor of her husband's face.

In answer he squeezed her arm and said, "I shall be back shortly."

Freddy accompanied him to see the king. Louis XVIII was surprisingly gracious to the two men, even going so far as to express concern over the colonel's pallor as well. Then, after informing them that the court left for Roye within the week, Louis rather curtly dismissed them.

Leverton went out early the next day for a walk about the town while Jason expressed himself content to sit in the parlor of the house where they were quartered with his wife and Eleanor. They were doing so when Talleyrand arrived. Milford immediately started to rise and Talleyrand waved him back into his seat. "*Mais non*, Colonel Milford. You have been injured and are still far from well, as one can clearly see. Please be comfortable. Madame, mademoiselle, I am enchanted to make your acquaintance," Talleyrand added as Milford introduced Lydia and Eleanor.

The two women curtsied and then Lydia said, "Shall we leave the room, monsieur?"

"No, no," Talleyrand said amiably, spreading his hands wide. "It is not necessary. I have no secrets to impart to your husband. I merely wished to assure myself he is suffering no ill effects from his journey and to welcome you to Cambrai. Though I much fear you will have little time to enjoy it before we leave for Roye."

"How soon?" Lydia could not help but ask with an anxious glance toward her husband.

Again Talleyrand spread his hands. "A day or two, perhaps. Not much more. Ah, you are distressed. But, madame, you are fortunate you were not with the king at Mons."

"Why?" Milford asked quietly, aware that Talleyrand said nothing without a purpose.

"You might have—no, would have—been awakened by a summons to rise in the early hours of the morning and prepare yourself for travel at once!" At the startled looks of the ladies Talleyrand said earnestly, "I swear it is true. Myself, I was forced to rise from my bed, dress more quickly than ever I have in my life, and drive as quickly as I could to see the king. I found him already in his carriage and preparing to go."

"But why?" Eleanor asked when Talleyrand stopped talking.

With a smile belied by the grim look in his eyes, Talleyrand bowed to her and replied, "Ah, mademoiselle, that was my fault. I was so tired from my journey that when I arrived in Mons I made the hideous error of believing it better to rest and present myself to the king in the morning in good order than to rush to present myself in all my dirt and dust and fatigue. His majesty was greatly offended. So greatly that I found myself dismissed from his service and the court on its way here that very night."

Naturally Lydia and Eleanor had no notion what to reply. Colonel Milford, however, knew the man somewhat better, and after a moment he said quietly, "Yet you are here, in his majesty's service."

Talleyrand inclined his head. "My duty is to France, as is the king's," he said. "You may tell the Duke of Wellington that I have said so, and that whatever differences may separate myself from his majesty, they will do so only temporarily."

Milford nodded and leaned back. This was what Talleyrand had come for. Nevertheless, he ventured to ask the Frenchman, "I have heard of the proclamation that was issued yesterday. You will forgive me if I say that I seemed to detect your hand in that."

Talleyrand inclined his head again.

"I am amazed the Comte d'Artois and the Duc de Berry did not dissuade the king from issuing it," Milford went on, after a moment.

Now Talleyrand smiled in a way that made Eleanor shiver. "They were not pleased," he said in reply. "But fortunately common sense prevailed and his majesty followed the advice of cooler heads. A thousand pities he is not always so wise."

A few minutes later the Frenchman took his leave, advising Lydia, as he did so, to take good care of her husband.

"I shall," Lydia replied, "and you were very kind to come and call upon him. I am afraid the journey was a trifle harder on him than he will admit."

Talleyrand bowed and was gone.

A few minutes later, as Milford was composing a report to Wellington and Lydia and Eleanor were discussing the visit, Freddy returned.

"Hallo, what's this? Have I missed something?" Leverton asked amiably.

"Only a visit from the illustrious Talleyrand himself," Eleanor retorted, equally amiably.

"Indeed?" Freddy asked, instantly serious as he took a seat. "The man appears to be quite formidable. Was there a reason for his visit? Or shouldn't I ask?"

Milford waved a hand negligently. "Oh, he wished to call upon me and welcome me to the entourage. All amiable and sociable. And, as usual, with a message beneath it for us English."

Leverton raised an expressive eyebrow, then said quizzically, "I suppose you know that his influence with the king is as great as it ever was."

"I do." Milford nodded. "The allies are inclined to believe that Talleyrand is here because they forced his presence upon the king. Talleyrand took pains to let me know it is not true."

Freddy spoke quietly. "One cannot go anywhere without hearing about the deliberations of the king's council these past few days. You know about the proclamation the king issued here. Well, I am told that Artois and Berry made a spirited attack on the proclamation. And upon Talleyrand, who introduced it, only to have his majesty inform them that he alone decides what may be said or not said at council meetings. What I suppose Talleyrand did not tell you is that he has been pressing hard for Louis to delay his entry into Paris."

"But why?" Eleanor could not help asking.

Freddy turned to her, a triumphant grin upon his face. "Because he does not wish Louis to enter the city as part of the force of foreigners. He would prefer to have Louis enter on his own, as though by right of birth to take his place as King of France."

"And Louis' answer to Talleyrand's advice?" Milford asked, leaning forward.

"Absolutely implacable," Freddy replied. "Louis means to enter Paris as soon as it is possible to do so, with foreigners or without them. He will not wait."

Milford leaned back in his chair, unable to suppress a small sound of satisfaction. "Good fellow, Freddy! I knew you would come in useful if I brought you. I shall have a message ready for Wellington directly. Will you take it?"

"Of course," Leverton retorted amiably.

"Is it safe?" Eleanor could not help but ask.

"Safe?" Freddy shrugged carelessly as he said, "I should think so. The road is well-traveled by British troops just now. Not a Bonapartist to be seen. Which reminds me," he added, turning to Milford, "the latest rumor is that Napoleon is headed for Cherbourg, where he means to take ship to America with a great deal of French gold."

"Indeed?" Milford asked skeptically.

"Well, there are other rumors, of course," Leverton conceded. "Most of which involve Napoleon's flight from Paris and a great deal of gold and some seaport or other. I simply gave you the version most newly arrived."

"Thank you," Milford said dryly. "I shall rate the information at its worth. Now you must excuse me while I compose that report for Wellington."

19

By July 3, Louis XVIII and his entourage arrived at Roye. The rumors continued to swirl about concerning Napoleon. Was he at Cherbourg? Was it his brother Joseph, instead? Was it all a feint to make the British think Napoleon meant to sail for America while in reality he was trying to raise an army somewhere else?

In addition, Talleyrand was still weaving his plans, now causing an uproar by suggesting that even those who had voted for the death of Louis XVI be allowed the serve the new government of France. By the time the retinue reached Saint-Denis, a day or so later, Wellington and Talleyrand had arranged, using Milford and Leverton to send or carry the messages, where and how Fouché should be approached.

"Fouché?" Lydia asked, wrinkling her nose at the unfamiliar name. "Who is he?"

Colonel Milford regarded his wife affectionately for a long moment before he answered. He had no fear that she would betray the confidence and at last he said, "The Duc d'Otrante. He is a regicide, a schemer, traitor, or hero depending upon one's point of view, and probably the key to the king's peaceful entry into Paris." He paused, then added with a sigh, "Matters could so easily grow into a violent confrontation. There are those who still support Napoleon and who believe that if they cannot have him they will at least have his son. Others, including the Czar Alexander, want the Duc d'Orleans upon the throne. And, of course, there are those who support Louis the Eighteenth."

"What will happen?" Lydia asked with some concern. "More fighting?"

"Not if we are fortunate; not if Talleyrand does his part with the French and Wellington his with the allies. Fouché, as head of police, can help a great deal as well," Milford said quietly. "But I will not deny that the first few days and weeks will be critical ones for France."

"Which is why," Lydia said fondly, "your role here is so important to Wellington. You are his eyes and ears in the French court, and I am all puffed up in my conceit as a consequence."

Since nothing could be more unlike the gentle nature of his wife, Colonel Milford laughed and said, "If I am the eyes and ears, then Freddy is the hands and feet, without whom I would be of little use! By the by, where is Freddy, anyway?"

"Gone for a walk with Nora," Lydia replied with a dimpled smile.

Milford was not deceived. "Are you matchmaking, my love?" he asked, pulling her onto his lap.

"Well-l, perhaps a little," she confessed. "Do you dislike it?"

"Not in the least," Milford replied with a smile.

"I have long thought Freddy needed a wife to steady him, and I like Miss Redmond. I think they would suit very well. Just don't forget, my love, that it is not my consent that is required, it is her father's."

"I shan't," Lydia replied. She hesitated, then asked, "Do you think Lord Redmond will give his consent? In London it was said they turned down any number of offers for her hand because they wished to hold out for an earl or a viscount or a duke."

"Perhaps you misjudge them and Miss Redmond simply did not wish to marry the gentlemen. But even were the worst of the gossip true," Milford replied quietly, "that was in London and before Miss Redmond ran away to Brussels with you. I think even Lord and Lady Redmond must realize by now they can no longer afford to disdain reasonable offers for her hand."

With a tiny sigh, Lydia snuggled closer to her husband's chest and said, "I do hope so, Jason. I think Nora and Freddy would be very happy together."

With a chuckle Milford replied, "If, my love, Freddy and Miss Redmond come to the same conclusion that you have, I doubt very much that Lord or Lady Redmond could keep them apart. They are both remarkably resourceful, you know."

At that moment Eleanor and Leverton were walking along the side of a small road. "What will happen when we get to Paris?" she asked.

"I imagine there will be some sort of procession through the streets of the city so that everyone may see that Louis the Eighteenth has returned as King of France," Leverton replied lightly. "We may go in a quieter way, if that is what Jason wishes and can arrange. And as soon as that is done, I think you will find that all the world flocks to Paris."

"What about Beauvais?" Eleanor asked reluctantly. "Will he be there as well?"

"I don't know," Freddy said honestly. "He was not with the king in Ghent nor, when Louis was in London, did the king ever extend his warmth to Beauvais. So it is unlikely there will be a royal command for him to appear. And unless he has drastically altered his situation, it may be that Beauvais will avoid Paris because he hasn't the funds to enjoy the city."

"That has never stopped him before," Eleanor pointed out dryly. She paused, then added quietly, "Beauvais' family was once part of the aristocracy. Surely after he regains his inheritance he will be welcome at court. I am afraid that if we are still in Paris I shall have to face him all over again, and I am not certain I can bear it."

For several long moments Leverton studied the young woman beside him. Eleanor's face was lined with the strain of the past few weeks, he noted, and the worry of the moment. And yet it seemed to him that the lines of worry were somehow far more endearing than her carefree smile had been when she was the toast of London. Without realizing he was doing so, Freddy reached out toward her and silently Eleanor moved into his arms. A moment later found her head against his shoulder and his lips upon hers, gently at first and then urgent with a need that rose in both of them.

When at last he let go of her, Freddy's first

words to Eleanor were, "I shall marry you, you know."

Eleanor pulled free and backed away from Leverton. "Shouldn't I have anything to say about the matter?" she asked, flushing. "Or are you roasting me?"

Amused and puzzled, Leverton said quizzically, "Roasting you? Now, how the devil did you arrive at that conclusion?"

"What else am I to think?" Eleanor asked quietly. "You have not once spoken of love or any other feelings. I could only imagine that you found me an amusing game or some such thing. And now you blithely say you mean to marry me."

Gently, without haste, Freddy drew her into his arms again. "Will all the words in the world make a difference to how I feel?" he asked the top of her head. "Would you believe me any more sincere if I swore undying love? Because I do love you and want to marry you."

"Oh, Freddy, I—"

Before Eleanor could complete her words, the sound of a small carriage interrupted them. Hastily Freddy pulled Eleanor to the side of the road as the coach wheels rolled by them, missing the pair by no more than a foot.

When it was gone, Freddy spoke. "This is not the time nor the place for me to speak to you of how I feel. And I suppose we should recollect that there is your family and mine to consider, though I'll stand warrant mine will be happy to hear I've a *tendre* for you. Certainly it is something Lydia has said she hoped for. But your family is another matter. They may think I do not rank highly enough or that I have not inherited a sufficiently large portion. I must speak to your father. That is, if you wish me to speak with your father?"

The last was spoken as a question, and with all her heart Eleanor replied, "Yes."

Leverton, who had drawn her to the side of the road when the carriage passed by, now let go of Eleanor's shoulders. Instead, he took her hand and said, "Whatever your father says, I will make him see reason. But will you be patient until all this furor is over and we may return to England?"

Silently Eleanor nodded, and the characteristic quirk of a smile once more upon his lips, Freddy said boyishly, "I think I had best take you back to the inn before we forget ourselves all over again."

Not letting go of his arm, Eleanor nodded and together they went back, careful to talk of neutral matters along the way. There Leverton told his sister she might begin to think in terms of a wedding and then sought out his brother-in-law, who was, as usual, composing a message for Wellington.

Meanwhile, Wellington and Fouché and Talleyrand prepared for the coming dinner to be given at Neuilly by the Englishman upon which so much depended. And Pozzo di Borgo pondered the meaning of his invitation to attend and just what message he would send his master, the Czar Alexander.

The Baron de Vitrolles called upon the Comte d'Artois to receive his final instructions from that fellow.

"I wish to know at once if that creature, Fouché, is made an offer by the devil Talleyrand," Artois told Vitrolles. "Even if it means you must wait in the corridors outside Monsieur Talleyrand's rooms until he returns tonight from the dinner party. I must know what has transpired!"

Virtolles bowed. "It shall be as you wish," he promised grimly.

In the end, however, nothing was quite as anyone wished. Neither Talleyrand nor Fouché would tell Vitrolles what had transpired at the dinner, and the ultraroyalists were forced to watch with anger as Louis XVIII received the man, a day or so later, to accept his pledge of fealty.

And on July 8 the King of France entered Paris by the avenue of kings, the Rue Saint-Denis. But even he could not fail to note the subdued manner in which he was greeted. Some said that it was precisely in anticipation of this reception that Talleyrand slipped into the city via another route and went straight to his own home in the Rue Saint-Florentin.

Likewise, Milford, who was still feeling the effects of travel, quietly entered Paris with his party by still a third route.

Napoleon might be gone but he was quite evidently not forgotten. It was a lesson that Wellington, with his sharp eyes and mind, was not likely to miss. And at his headquarters in Paris it was a message he took great pains to impress upon his still-diminished staff as he met with them that afternoon. "I've no desire," he told his men bluntly, "to have to put down an uprising by an outraged populace. So exercise tact and care whenever possible in dealing with the citizens here. Is that understood?"

His men knew him too well to do other than agree.

20

Monsieur Henri Dubois looked about the small parlor of the inn and with a nod of satisfaction to himself took a seat. He then loudly ordered a bottle of wine, put his feet up on an adjacent chair, and proceeded to wait. It was far less than an hour later when he learned what he wanted to know. And at that point he was surrounded by a half-dozen of the local citizenry, all of whom were extremely appreciative of Monsieur Dubois' generosity.

He was still sitting there when the Comte de Beauvais entered the tavern. Beauvais walked with a swagger and seated himself as far away as possible from the other local folks. There was some grumbling but nothing said loud enough that their new landlord might overhear. As Dubois had already ascertained, Beauvais had been granted his land. Minus, of course, taxes and what had been sold to pay for those over the past years of Napoleon's reign or given to men who had served him and somehow contrived not to lose their positions even with the change of power.

And yet, Dubois noted, Beauvais did not look happy. Indeed, there was almost a harassed air about the man as he drank his aperitif. With a shrug in the count's direction Dubois asked his companions, "What problem?"

One of the men snickered then spat. "*Bâtard!* That one is angry because our local *fille de joie*, after one encounter, refuses to service him." At Dubois' look of surprise the fellow leaned closer and said softly, "It is said that what he wants, that one, is so depraved that even money cannot tempt the girl. Nor has she any need. There is not a person in the village, not even the oh-so-virtuous wives, who would not gladly pay for her food and shelter rather than see her please such an animal."

"Pig!" another Frenchman said, but quietly. "To have one of those Beauvais back again after the emperor promised we would not is unspeakable."

"Napoleon is emperor no longer," Dubois replied softly, "now Louis is king again."

"I tell you, my friend," the first one said gravely, "that the English devil Wellington may have defeated the emperor, but never again will we allow the kings of France to rule us as they once did. Truly their age is past and the time, now, when we must say so in whispers will soon pass as well."

Dubois did not deny it. In the days he had spent traveling to reach this village he had seen and heard much. What the man before him said and the others nodded agreement to was only an echo of words whispered in every other tavern he had stopped at. Which should not be a surprise, he thought grimly to himself, otherwise Napoleon would not have found his return from Elba so easy

178

or his support so strong. Dubois wondered if the great men who ran their nations—British, Prussian, Russian, or French—understood that truth as well as these peasants did. It was one more piece of information to be passed on to Colonel Milford. But carefully, oh, so carefully. The English were known to be temperamental and Dubois had no wish to be thrown out on his ear; rather, he looked for a bonus from all this.

After a few more minutes, a few more questions, Dubois rose and paid his shot to the innkeeper, then asked for his horse to be brought around. It was as he was preparing to mount that the rider came galloping into the courtyard calling for Beauvais. Quietly Dubois signaled for the groom to take his horse back to the stables and in the wake of the new arrival Dubois reentered the inn.

In Paris there was a great deal of confusion, but Lydia Milford found that, as in Brussels, Jason smoothed the way and hired a house for her. Even more helpful, from her point of view, was that attention had turned from Nora to Lady Frances Wedderburn-Webster and the Duke of Wellington's attachment to that lady. Thus far, the conjectures were spoken in a whisper, but they were nevertheless spoken.

Indeed, the Duke of Wellington had become the cause for a great deal of speculation and comment. His victory at Waterloo was not forgotten. Rather, it was the source of some of the discontent. He was not sufficiently proud in his bearing or assertive in his speech, some complained. Lady Shelley was heard to protest that he ought to want the cheers of his men instead of suffering them with distaste. Or that

Wellington was too self-effacing in his conversations except when they were about those dismal subjects of war and politics. And how could he endure, much less seek out the company of that abhorrent woman, Madame Craufurd, the grandmother of the Count d'Orsay? He neither understood nor wished to accept his importance, Lady Shelley and others complained, and as a result, the consequence of all the British *ton* in Paris was diminished.

Lydia Milford could not be expected to agree. Perhaps because of Jason and through him her glimpses of the true nature of war, Lydia found Wellington's demeanor admirable. He did not force himself or his views upon the French king, as he might have done after the victory at Waterloo, but was content to grant the emerging government as much autonomy as possible. Indeed, when he did interfere, it was often at the behest of Talleyrand. Wellington understood, perhaps better than anyone, that in days like these, at the end of one war, were often sown the seeds of future wars. And as he had quietly confided to Colonel Milford, the time was coming when France and England would need to be allies and not enemies.

For Eleanor politics were secondary to the heady experience of finding herself in Paris. Particularly since Frederick Leverton was amiable enough to indulge her wish to play tourist and visit all the sights of the city. John Witton had also arrived and he or Lydia often came along as well, for Jason was involved, at least peripherally, with the Paris peace conference, which opened on July 12.

To be sure, there was no repetition of the scene between Nora and Freddy that had occurred at

Saint-Denis, nor even a chance for the pair to be alone to speak of it. But there was a warmth between the pair and an unspoken closeness visible to everyone who saw them together. And if they did not speak of love, at least Freddy was always willing to speak to Eleanor of everything else, including politics.

No one quite knew what was happening that summer in Paris. Nominally the people had accepted Louis XVIII's presence in the city as well as the allies, and most were even willing to cheer the military parades. But there was also undeniably a sense of reserve about them, almost as though they were waiting to hear if Napoleon would yet again escape his would-be captors. Rumors abounded, from the return of the emperor to the notion that the allies intended to strip Paris of its art treasures and send them back to the countries from which they had come.

Meanwhile, the British *ton* spent its time in shopping at all the fashionable salons that had been forbidden to them for the past few months, riding in the parks, and calling upon one another, and in giving and attending parties. In short, much the same thing they would have been doing had they been in London. There were picnics where Catalani or Grassini or Tom Moore sang. At other times Kemble discussed Shakespeare while Walter Scott talked about Madame de Pompadour.

To one such picnic the Milfords, Eleanor, Leverton, and Witton were all invited. Lydia had her cook prepare a large hamper of food and the party set out in two carriages. This one was being held on the grounds of the Louvre and given in honor—of course—of Wellington. The duke was in an amiable mood and inclined to wander from party to party, sharing a little of each one's cheer. Lady Shelley was accompanying him on his rounds and most evidently trying to cajole him into letting her ride one of his horses. Preferably the horse he rode at Waterloo.

"Well, perhaps on the twenty-fifth," Wellington allowed at last. "You may ride with me when we hold the grand review at Saint-Denis. But mind, no boasting about the favor. I don't wish to be beseiged by every lady in Paris who will otherwise feel slighted."

Lady Shelley smiled sweetly. "I should not dare to cross such a forceful commander as yourself. Nor should I like to think myself the cause of anyone plaguing you at all."

"Nevertheless, madame, you shall be," Wellington replied curtly. "Don't you agree, Mrs. Milford?" he asked Lydia as he reached their party.

"Most certainly," Lydia said promptly. Then, after a judicious pause, she added, "May I know what it is that I have just agreed with?"

Everyone laughed and Wellington turned his hand in the air. "It doesn't signify," he told Lydia kindly. "Merely a slight disagreement between Lady Shelley and myself. But nothing of importance and it is infamous of me to tease you so." He paused, then greeted the others there. "Hallo, Miss Redmond. I understand that you and Mrs. Milford are the ones I have to thank for the restoration of Colonel Milford to my staff. It is a debt I assure you I shall not soon forget."

The duke might have spoken lightly but there was no doubt as to the strain in his eyes. Nor could one doubt that he was thinking of the men he had lost at Waterloo. Then he abruptly squared his shoulders and went on, "Hallo, Leverton. Good to see you again. And Mr. Witton, is it not? How do you do, sir? Enjoying Paris?"

"It is a most interesting city," Witton replied. "The museums alone are extraordinary."

"Yes, because the French under that barbarian Napoleon looted all the rest of Europe to fill them," Lady Shelley burst out in protest.

Wellington lifted a hand in a peace-making gesture but Witton merely nodded gravely. "Quite true," he said quietly. "Nevertheless, however reprehensible the methods, the result is a city filled with exquisite treasures."

"Of more than one sort," Leverton said, a quirk of a smile upon his face. "There is at least one dancer in the city that one must call a treasure."

"Freddy!" Lydia protested in outrage while the gentlemen all laughed.

Lady Shelley quirked an eyebrow at Lydia and said with a mock sigh of resignation, "Men! Do they ever grow up, I wonder?"

"Never!" Wellington retorted, a twinkle in his eyes.

That brought a round a protest as well, and a few moments later the duke moved on to converse with another party of friends. Lady Shelley stayed with the Milfords. Meanwhile, Colonel James Stanhope wandered about, reciting from Byron's *Childe Harold*.

Reluctantly, some hours later, the merrymakers returned to their respective lodgings, everyone in the most excellent of humors. As they entered the foyer of the house Colonel Milford had rented, the majordomo greeted the colonel with the news that he had a visitor. "I have set him in the, er,

183

bookroom," the majordomo explained with a cough.

"Thank you, Jacques," Jason replied. "I shall go in to him directly. Did he give a name?"

Jacques' face was rigid with disapproval as he answered. "No, sir, he did not. He merely kept insisting that you would want to see him."

"Shall I come with you?" Leverton asked his brother-in-law quietly.

Milford hesitated only an instant before he said, "Yes, do, Freddy. I can always send you out if the business is private, but I mistrust a man who will not give his name, and I may have need of you."

The two men made their excuses to the ladies and went to the small room given over, by the previous resident, to books. Upon opening the door, Milford paused in surprise at the sight of his caller and Leverton's hand tightened on the door-jamb. A moment later both men had recovered and moved forward, closing the door behind themselves.

"We had begun to give up hope of seeing you, Dubois," Milford said easily.

The Belgian shrugged. "What would you? I could not take the time to post you notices of my progress, I had a count to find."

"And did you find him?" Leverton asked, his voice taut with emotion.

Dubois mopped his brow and did not at once speak. But when he did, the words seemed to tumble out as though Dubois could not speak them fast enough. "*Oui monsieur*. I have just come from the village where is located the estate of the Comte de Beauvais. But first I had to track him many places before he came to Paris, and here I lost him. Eventually I learned he had left the city

and I followed again and found him at the estate,''
Dubois explained. He paused, then added,
spreading his hands wide in a deprecating gesture,
"You will pardon, I hope, that I came here. The
other gentleman, Monsieur Witton, was not at his
lodgings and I heard you had hired this house,
Monsieur. Also, I did not give my name because I
have not the ambition to be everywhere known.
Each person who hears one name is someone who
may contradict when he later hears me called by
another.''

Milford bowed toward Dubois. Leverton could
scarcely contain his impatience though nothing
showed in his face or voice as he said carelessly,
"Yes, but what have you learned about the
count?"

"Ah, the Comte de Beauvais!" Dubois said with
a malicious grin. "He will not find it easy, that
one, to regain his inheritance. Not in the ordinary
course of things.''

"But I thought he had," Leverton said,
straightening up.

"Yes, formally," Dubois conceded. "But the
peasants, ah, that is another matter. They are
most reluctant to accept him in their midst. The
memories of that family are not, I comprehend,
very pleasant. Nor is this count held in great
regard. He will have a battle, that one, to assert his
authority. The people will fight him in a thousand
little ways and I cannot blame them. He is, you
will pardon, a pig.''

Leverton shrugged and said generously, "Of
course.''

Disconcerted, Dubois lost the train of his
thoughts, but after a moment he recovered and
went on. "He was most desolated when I saw him.

Even the *fille de joie* of the village will not attend to him. There are, I think, much exaggerated tales of his depravity but," Dubois concluded with a shrug of his own, "so it goes."

"Yes, but will he give up his plans?" Milford asked with a frown.

"That one? No. To him it is a matter of honor, and he does not retreat," Dubois replied with a snort of contempt. "Besides, he is not so comfortable with the funds that he can afford to leave. I understand he does not yet pay his bill at the tavern, which is but one more reason he is despised." Dubois paused, sighed heavily, then said, "There is something more. The day I left I saw someone arrive to see the count. A man I have often heard spoken of as a creature of the Duc d'Orléans. I have spoken to some who say that the Comte de Beauvais' father was one of those executed in the plot to assassinate Bonaparte in 1804, so one would think he would support the king. But I have heard elsewhere that he is angry because the king never acknowledged this service. At any rate, Beauvais and the other gentleman spoke in private, but because of what I have heard elsewhere, I believe the Comte de Beauvais may be involved in a plot to seize control of France for the Duc d'Orléans and execute all those who ever cooperated with Bonaparte."

"Is that possible?" Milford asked.

"Perhaps. Perhaps not," Dubois replied with a shrug. "But what is certain is that one may have much blood spilled in the effort to do so."

"There has certainly been no indication that Beauvais is in favor with the Bourbons. Quite the contrary, in fact. I understand he was only once received by Louis the Eighteenth in England," Leverton said thoughtfully.

"And this village? Where precisely is it?" Milford asked Dubois, spreading out a map.

Dubois rose, went over to the desk, and began to trace with his finger the best route to the village where Beauvais was to be found. As he did so, he said, "The village is a little north and west of the city of Beauvais, and the route I give you is not, you understand, the shortest way, but it is the safest. There are still those in France who would delight in bringing low a British soldier. Or," he added with a sharp look at Leverton, "any Englishman at all. There are many who still believe that Napoleon was the savior of France and will not soon forgive those who brought him down. Particularly now, when there are rumors everywhere and some believe he is soon to return and others that he is soon to be hanged by the British. Be careful."

"We shall. And thank you, Dubois," Colonel Milford replied, pulling out the agreed-upon money to pay the fellow. He then added some more to the amount. "A bonus," he explained, "for your information as to the mood of the people and for the count's special activities. That is something good for us to know."

Dubois bowed. "*Merci*," he said. "You are a gentleman, truly. And now I go, but should I discover anything new, I return at once."

Milford nodded. "Yes, thank you. You have been of the greatest assistance. Freddy, show the fellow out, will you?"

With a quizzical smile at his brother-in-law Leverton did so, asking a few more whispered questions of his own on the way to the outer door.

When he returned to the bookroom, Leverton found Milford still deep in thought. "Well, Jason? When do we leave?"

Startled, the colonel looked at his brother-in-law. After a moment he said thoughtfully, "Not until after I have spoken with Wellington, certainly. I think he will be very interested to hear what Dubois had to say. Then, Freddy, we shall see."

21

In the end, Colonel Milford and Leverton traveled to Beauvais' village together. When Witton offered to come along as well, Milford replied, "I am grateful for your offer, John, but the fewer of us who go, the better. And I should like you to do me the favor of looking in upon Miss Redmond and my wife from time to time while we are gone."

"Of course," Witton replied gravely with half a bow.

"Thank you," Milford said quietly. "I shall tell Lydia and Miss Redmond that you are nearby if needed, though I do not expect you will be."

"Of course," Witton repeated. Then, with some concern he asked, "Are you ready to travel and take on a mission such as this? Couldn't the Duke of Wellington send someone else?"

Freddy laughed and there was a touch of reproof in his voice as he said, "Try to get Jason to admit that, John. I cannot do so."

Milford favored his brother-in-law with a withering look, then turned to Witton. "I am perfectly recovered," he said. "As for Wellington sending someone else, I didn't want him to. I've as much experience in this sort of thing as anyone, and besides, we hope, if it is possible, to retrieve the rest of Miss Redmond's letters. You must see that we would not want a stranger along for that."

He paused, then went on more mildly, "It's past time I returned to duty. This peace conference doesn't count. And in any event, I am taking Freddy with me. Wellington agrees that for this sort of mission it can be an advantage to have someone who is not known as a military man. If Beauvais does discover we are about, he will assume it is because of Miss Redmond and we may catch him off guard. And now we must be going. If Dubois is correct in his suspicions, there is no time to lose. An uprising by Orléanists would be disastrous just now."

"But so far away?" Witton protested. "What can it matter if in some obscure village a count declares himself for Orléans?"

"The village may be obscure," Milford replied dryly, "but the city of Beauvais is not. And our count is close enough that he could easily lead a small force there and capture the city. That would matter, I assure you. It is a center of manufacturing, you know."

In spite of himself Leverton laughed and said, "Somehow I cannot imagine Beauvais as the head of a military action. I should more easily imagine him quaking under the bed as the troops marched by."

"Perhaps there is more to the man than we know," Milford replied quietly, "or perhaps there is some other service Beauvais is expected to perform. For example, he need only hide soldiers on his estate until someone else can lead them into the city for the damage to be done. That is part of what you and I must find out."

"Does Lydia know?" Freddy asked abruptly.

Milford nodded. "Lydia knows where I am going and why," he said. "She cannot like it, but she will not carry on."

"I must still take my leave of Miss Redmond," Leverton said grimly.

Milford turned to Freddy. "Well, you had best do so quickly. We leave within the hour. Take very little—only what can be carried in a satchel on horseback. We travel light and we travel fast."

Freddy nodded and the three men left the room. Leverton found Eleanor in the drawing room arranging some flowers. As he walked in, she favored Freddy with a brilliant smile. Happily she said, "Oh, are you going out riding? You are dressed for it, I see."

Leverton hesitated only a moment, then he strode forward and took Eleanor's hand in his. "I came to take my leave of you," he said quietly. As dismay spread across her face, he hastened to reassure her. "I shall be back in a few days," he said.

Eleanor looked at him, a troubled expression upon her face as she said, just as quietly, "You are going with Colonel Milford, aren't you? A mission for Wellington, I collect. Not that Lydia told me so, but what else can it be?"

In spite of himself Freddy laughed, "Oh, a hundred things, I should think," he chided her playfully.

Eleanor shook her head and, tilting her chin up, said, "Not when Lydia looks as distracted as she does this morning. No, don't worry, I shan't plague you to tell me any more about it." She paused and added, with a ghost of a smile, "I collect it would be useless anyway. I only hope it is not dangerous."

Taking her other hand in his as well, Freddy said with a smile, "I shall take very good care of myself, I assure you, Miss Redmond. Can you doubt it when I have you to come back to?"

He leaned forward, about to kiss Eleanor, and she leaned forward to meet his lips with her own when they were interrupted by a loud cough behind them. Startled, the pair turned to find themselves regarded with disapproving eyes by Lady Shelley, who stood beside the footman who had come to announce her.

Hastily Eleanor and Freddy moved apart, Miss Redmond coloring becomingly. Clearing his own throat, Leverton turned to her and said formally, "Yes, well, Miss Redmond, I shall see you later, then."

"Of course, Mr. Leverton," she replied with equal formality. "Lady Shelley, how do you do? Lydia will be delighted you are here. Pray sit down and I shall ring for some tea."

Quietly Leverton made good his escape.

The Comte de Beauvais, who was the cause of all this activity, was happily unaware of any of it. Instead, he was riding around the perimeter of his estate. It was a tour that took some time, even though the estate had greatly shrunk from what it had been before the revolution. Jean-Pierre found himself breathing deeply the air of home. How old had he been when he first left? It was a question the Comte de Beauvais could answer only because his mother had told him the story so often. His own memory was too jumbled, too full of the images that had been important to a child of five. He remembered being cold and hungry and angry because he was being bundled up in dirty blankets and the stable boy's clothes and told constantly to hush. His mother had been short-tempered and his father strangely silent. Their nurse had cried and then been gone. And *grand-père* had spent the night vowing to cut the throat of anyone who tried to stop them.

Even now the memory was enough to make Jean-Pierre shiver in the warm afternoon sun and bring him close to rage. It would take time but he would restore the family honor, of that Beauvais was determined. And exact revenge for all the petty insults his mother had been forced to swallow by the fine British ladies who had bought the hats she had made to support them when their money had run out in England. Already, with Lady Deerfield, Miss Redmond, and others, he had begun. Let them feel, for once, the sting of the sort of humiliation that had driven his mother to her grave. And even the king should regret that he had turned his back on Jean-Pierre's father. Had he offered Jean-Pierre's mother even the smallest of pensions, she would not have had to sell those cursed hats.

Little by little, Beauvais meant to regain the land that had once belonged to the family and erase every trace of evidence that the château had ever been used by anyone else.

Then and only then he would find a bride. Not because he wanted to, but because it was his duty as the last Beauvais to breed an heir. Otherwise, what he meant to do was in vain. And if the Duc d'Orléans triumphed in his plan, success would come all the sooner. He, Jean-Pierre, would personally see to the execution of the traitors who now held Beauvais land. And then he would go after all the other traitors hereabouts.

Grimly the Comte de Beauvais nodded. That was something he looked forward to doing. Abruptly he glanced toward the sky. It was getting late. Time to return to the house.

What none of them realized was that at the same time Colonel Milford was setting out for Beauvais' estate, Lady Redmond was already on her way from Calais to Paris. With, she had decided, one short detour to attend to certain matters concerning her daughter, Nora's, future. She meant to call upon the Comte de Beauvais and make it very clear to him that he was not to harass Nora ever again or she would see that he paid dearly for it. No doubt the man thought that, with Nora's family safely in England, he could threaten her in perfect safety. Well, now he would learn his mistake.

Lady Redmond had no fears for her own safety in calling upon the Comte de Beauvais. He might be a blackguard who delighted in trying to ruin young maidens, but even he would not go so far as violence. After all, he was a gentleman, of sorts. As for propriety, Lady Redmond did have her maid Penelope at hand, and in any event, she was a married woman, not some green girl just out of the schoolroom.

Upon hearing the news, at Amiens, that they were not going directly to Paris but that Lady Redmond meant to make a detour to a small village near the city of Beauvais, her maid, Penelope, let out a loud, low moan of protest.

"Oh, do stop that, Penelope," Lady Redmond

said impatiently. "This is precisely why I did not tell you my plans in England but have waited until now to do so. You are forever complaining about one thing or another."

"If you are not happy with me—" Penelope began with a distinct sniff.

Lady Redmond cut her short. "Nonsense!" she said forthrightly. "You have been with me for years and I do not underestimate your value, but I do wish you will cease this moaning. It cannot, after all, help anything. We are going to see the Comte de Beauvais, and that is that. Indeed, I should think you would be grateful we are off the water and on dry land."

With another distinct sniff Penelope answered her mistress, "And so I would be if this coach would cease to rock like a boat. It is impossible, I cannot endure this."

"Fustian," Lady Redmond said firmly. "You know you will be fine as soon as you have had some hot tea. And a good meal. You have scarcely eaten since we left England and that is why you are feeling so peakish."

At the talk of food Penelope turned, if possible, even paler. It was fortunate for the peace of the pair that for the next several minutes Lady Redmond sat engrossed in the passing countryside. Penelope did not feel like talking.

Meanwhile, a letter was reaching Eleanor from her sister. Amanda had written it as soon as she knew her mother's plans, even before Lady Redmond set out for Paris. But the mails were most irregular these days between England and the Continent and it had taken it some time to reach Eleanor. Still, in the end, it did arrive.

* * *

The firelight flickered on the face of the Frenchman who stood in the private parlor of the inn. He addressed the Englishman in execrable English. "Monsieur, the count, he was vairy agreable. He give the orders that I am to be let in and all marches well. Not the surprise, he tells me all the things, all the plans. Understand, I am amazed. And when he says that I am expected, I leave vairy quickly. *Tout de suite*, in fact."

"Jason, your disguise is marvelous. Not even your own mother would know you or guess that you were not a Frenchman, but pray spare me the fractured English," Leverton said dryly. "Instead, sit down and tell me properly what happened at the château."

The "Frenchman" nodded and did as he was bid, straddling a chair to face the other man. "Very well. I went to the château and asked to speak with Beauvais. I was shown in at once, told that the count was expecting me, and offered refreshment. In less than two minutes I was in the study and in conversation with Beauvais. From his manner it was clear that he was expecting someone and assumed I was the person expected. I did nothing to change his opinion. Beauvais spoke of the Duc d'Orléans and of revenge against those who had supported Bonaparte or supported too actively the revolution. I asked Beauvais if he had anyone particular in mind and he mentioned the neighboring landowners who hold, I gather, what was once Beauvais land. So then I asked his opinions of the British. He assumed it was a sort of test and said that they would soon be gone from France. Most important, he is expecting a band of troops, cutthroats more likely, to come and be quartered at his household."

"But I don't understand," Freddy said impatiently. "If his father was such an ardent royalist, why was he supporting Orléans?"

"I asked him that," Milford said with a quirk of his eyebrows. "It turns out Dubois was quite right. I said there were those who questioned the loyalty of a man whose father died for Louis the Eighteenth. He said that it was because of that, because the king had never acknowledged his father's sacrifice and death in his service, that Beauvais was determined to help in his overthrow."

"What, now?" Freddy asked.

"I shall be riding straight back to Paris to report to Wellington. Time is important, since I gather from Beauvais that some sort of action is planned for three days from today and Wellington and Talleyrand must be warned."

Milford paused and Leverton said seriously, "Let me go instead."

Milford shook his head. "The duke will be expecting me. Officially I am here on my own and Wellington is shrugging off any suggestions that there is more to it than that. But the truth is he will be well aware of the importance of the message I carry and I must give it to him myself. There are things I do not wish to tell even to you, and besides, I am the one who has spoken with Beauvais, I am the one who will have the answers to the questions Wellington is certain to ask." He paused, then added, "I suspect he would like nothing better than to catch men like Beauvais in the act of harboring Orléanists because then he could do something about them, possibly bring them up on charges."

"I cannot like it," Leverton said with a frown, "but I also know you too well to think I can stop you. Do you leave tonight?"

Milford shook his head decisively. "No. With these unsettled times I am too likely to be shot at, by our side or theirs, at night, and I can't risk the message not getting through. I only wish I dared ride harder and faster."

At once Leverton expressed his concern. "Are you all right, Jason?"

The colonel waved a careless hand. There was a ghost of a smile upon his face as he replied, "Well enough. It is not my health that will slow me down but caution. After all, I do not wish to advertise the fact that I carry important information; I should prefer to appear a harmless traveler. But I will leave at dawn."

Leverton nodded. "I trust you have no objection if I stay?"

"That depends upon what you mean to do after I am gone," Milford said coolly.

"I shall call upon Beauvais in the morning," Leverton answered quietly, "and retrieve everything that belongs to Miss Redmond. Since I understand that you do not wish him to suspect how much we know of his other activities, I shall pretend my only concern is Miss Redmond and I shall say to him that if he ever so much as whispers a rumor abroad about her, I shall kill him. I think he will see reason."

"Isn't that dangerous?" Milford asked with some concern. "What if he threatens you?"

Freddy opened his coat. "I have brought a pair of pistols, and with what you have told me, I should have no hesitation in doing what needs to be done." At his brother-in-law's stunned expression Freddy laughed, a trifle shakily. "No, no, I do not mean to murder the fellow," he said. "But he strikes me as a man very easy to frighten and he need only think that I mean to do so."

"That is something of a relief," Milford said dryly. "I should hate to have to explain to Lydia why her brother was being hanged for murder. I am still concerned, mind you, for I think the count a dangerous man. But as I don't know how to stop you, I'll settle for carrying my message to Wellington. Meanwhile, shall we have one last glass of wine to toast the success of our separate ventures?"

22

Eᴀʀʟʏ ᴛʜᴇ ɴᴇxᴛ morning, Lady Redmond's carriage pulled into the courtyard of the only tavern or inn in the village near Beauvais' château. Immediately the innkeeper came out into the yard, bowing to the lady who leaned out of her coach to ask directions. "*Le Comte de Beauvais? Mais, oui, certainement,*" he said. "His house, it is very easy to find, I will give directions to your driver. But first, would you like some refreshment? A little bread and cheese, perhaps?"

"*Non, merci,*" Lady Redmond said with a shake of her head. "But thank you for your help."

She listened as he gave directions to her driver, then directed her coachman to give the innkeeper some coins in thanks. A few minutes later, they were on their way to the château.

Meanwhile, Freddy Leverton had not yet risen from his bed, though Colonel Milford had ridden away at dawn.

Penelope was still complaining. "I do not see," she said, "why we must travel so swiftly that one's insides become all jumbled. Surely a more sedate pace would do just as well."

Lady Redmond looked with tolerant amusement at the woman who had been with her since her marriage so many years ago to Lord Redmond. Some would, she knew, have called it outrageous that she allowed a servant so much freedom to complain. But Penelope had stood by her without complaint when it mattered, and Lady Redmond felt she could afford to be tolerant now. Still, even she was relieved when they pulled around to the front of the count's chateau.

"I shall not be long," Lady Redmond told her maid and then the driver.

He nodded phlegmatically while Penelope merely shook her head in silent—for once—disapproval.

Lady Redmond sounded the knocker at the front door quite firmly and it was only a few moments before the door was opened.

"I am here from England to see the Comte de Beauvais," she said, purposely omitting her name.

If the fellow thought it unconventional that she should call upon a gentleman, alone, he did not say so. Nor did he object to her lack of a name. He merely bowed and indicated she should come in, and then he showed her to a well-appointed if a trifle dusty parlor. Only then did the fellow speak. "I shall inform the count you are here," he said.

Lady Redmond nodded curtly. "Pray do so at once," she said.

Left alone, Lady Redmond moved slowly about the room looking closely at the once-splendid furnishings and the now-defaced portraits of, she presumed, Beauvais' ancestors. As a result, her back was to the door when he entered the room and he did not at once recognize her.

As for the Comte de Beauvais, he had been returning from a morning ride when one of the grooms informed him that he had a visitor. Humming to himself, Beauvais had dismounted and briskly strode toward the house and the parlor where he was told the lady was waiting. "Madame?" he said, a question in his voice.

Lady Redmond turned and Beauvais' good humor turned swiftly to apprehension. A grim look replaced his polite smile as he waited for her to speak.

"Hello, Beauvais," she said coolly. "I notice you do not welcome me to France, but that is all of a piece with what one would expect of you. Or is it guilt that keeps you silent? I shall not speak of your wager concerning my daughter, for that is beyond discussing. Instead, I will tell you that I have heard of how you behaved in Brussels. That you were despicable enough to set about letters my misguided daughter wrote to you in confidence that, if you were a true gentleman, you would never have shown to anyone. I also suspect you of attempting to extort money from Nora by threatening to show them."

"And you are here to tell me what?" he asked, leaning lazily against a mantelpiece.

"I am here because I can only conclude that you have felt Nora had no one to protect her from behavior such as yours. You are wrong and I am here to tell you so," Lady Redmond replied.

"Indeed?" Beauvais laughed. "But what is it you mean to do? Call me out?"

"Don't be absurd," Lady Redmond retorted impatiently. "My husband need not call you out to bring you to account."

"You forget, madame, this is my country, not yours," Beauvais countered.

He would have said more but just then a servant

entered the room and spoke to the count. He, in turn, told Lady Redmond, "Your maid has taken ill. The coachman has driven her around back and she is in the kitchen with my staff if you wish to go to her."

"Yes, at once," Lady Redmond said, starting forward. She paused a moment, however, to add, "We shall continue this discussion later, monsieur."

The count merely bowed with great irony in his expression. Then he was alone and laughing silently to himself over the naïveté of this English lady that she thought she need only appear to cow him.

Very shortly after Lady Redmond's coach had pulled out of the courtyard of the village inn, another carriage had pulled in, at great speed. "*Sacrebleu*," the innkeeper exclaimed. "Never have we been so popular."

He watched as a lady and gentleman descended from that coach and somehow he was not surprised when he discovered that they were English as well. And when they, too, asked about the Comte de Beauvais, he merely shrugged fatalistically and gave directions to the château. With satisfaction the innkeeper noted the way the lady's lips pursed in disapproval and he heartily wished the count joy with his many visitors that morning.

The gentleman's next question startled him out of his reverie. "Do you have two Englishmen staying here?"

"We did, monsieur, but one left at dawn," the innkeeper replied. "The other one has not yet come down to breakfast."

Leverton, however, had been awakened by the commotion in the courtyard and now he poked his head out of his window and called down, "John Witton! What the devil are you doing here? And Miss Redmond?"

"Here to see you," Witton retorted gloomily. "And Miss Redmond wants to see her mother."

At these words a startled expression crossed Leverton's face and he replied, "Lady Redmond? What *are* you talking about? What would she be doing here?"

At this the innkeeper coughed and said, "Monsieur? You seek lady? English lady?"

"Yes, yes, we do," Eleanor replied instantly. "Is she here?"

The fellow shook his head. "She also asked how to reach the château of the Comte de Beauvais. This very morning."

At these words Eleanor grew pale and clutched Witton's arm as she said, "We have to go after her. At once!"

Gently he freed his arm and in a sensible voice said, "I think we had best discuss this inside and with Freddy. I daresay he wishes to speak with you."

Eleanor swallowed hard and nodded. She made no protest as she followed him into the inn. They waited downstairs and Leverton immediately joined them. Quickly Witton apprised him of the letter Eleanor had received from her sister Amanda.

"She said my mother meant to stop here and confront the count," Eleanor said anxiously. "She cannot understand how unscrupulous he is."

"On the contrary, I should say that it is because Lady Redmond does understand his nature that she is here," Witton countered in what was most evidently a repetition of an old argument.

"Forgive me," Freddy said grimly, "but I still do not understand why you are here."

A trifle bitterly Witton replied, "Because once Miss Redmond read her sister's letter, she was determined to come and see Beauvais."

"Only to find my mother. She may be in trouble," Eleanor retorted defensively.

With an exasperated sigh Witton retorted, "I doubt that very much."

"On the contrary," Freddy said quietly, "she may be. Jason discovered a great deal last night. But in any event, why did you agree to bring her, John? I would have thought you would have better sense than that."

From between clenched teeth Witton replied, "Miss Redmond was determined to come. With or without me. I could not make her see that there might be any danger to her. Nor could I let her come alone."

"Well, where is Lydia? Why didn't she stop Miss Redmond? Or failing that, come along herself?" Leverton asked in exasperation.

If possible, John Witton's face grew more dour still. "Because Miss Redmond waited until your sister was laid down in her bed, with a badly twisted ankle, dosed with laudanum, with orders from the doctor that she was under no circumstances to be disturbed or moved for at least twenty-four hours, to decide upon this mad scheme."

Immediately Eleanor leapt to her own defense. "That's not fair," she said hotly. "Amanda's letter came after Lydia hurt her ankle. And I truly didn't want to disturb her. That's why I purposely didn't tell her where I was going. I didn't want her to try to follow, not with her ankle twisted so badly."

"But you didn't mind leaving her to fend for herself?" Witton replied curtly. "Or letting her worry?"

To the man's further exasperation, Eleanor only laughed. "Now, that is doing it much too brown," she said good-naturedly. "You can scarcely say that in a house full of servants Lydia has been abandoned to fend for herself. As for letting her worry, how can she do that when she knows I am with you?"

Leverton broke into their conversation then, a smile beginning to twitch at the corners of his mouth. His voice was stern, however, as he said, "I understand your problem, John, and I thank you for accompanying Miss Redmond, in spite of how exasperating you must have found her." To Eleanor he said, ignoring her gasp of outrage, "You may have come this far, my love, but you will go no farther. John and I will go up to the château and confront Beauvais and see if your mother is there. And afterward you and I are going to have a very long talk."

"But—" she started to protest.

Leverton cut her short with a voice that would have done credit to his brother-in-law the colonel. "You will stay here or you will go back to Paris at once. And if we have any trouble from you about it, I shall personally give you the spanking you so richly deserve. Then I shall bind and gag you and take you straight back to Paris myself."

"You wouldn't dare!" Eleanor said with another gasp of outrage."

"Oh yes I would," Freddy said, taking a step toward her. "In the midst of war you would be surprised how little time there is to think of the proprieties."

"But we are not at war," Eleanor continued to protest, backing away.

"And I say that for the purpose at hand, we may as well be," Freddy said as he continued to advance on her. "There is more happening here than you can known. Much more is at stake than your mother's safety. And I will not risk your safety or anyone else's." Freddy waited until Eleanor lowered her eyes and then he asked, more gently, "Now, do you wait here for us or do I bind and gag you and send you back to Paris at once?"

Meekly Eleanor sat down. "I'll wait here," she said in a small voice.

"Good," Witton said curtly. "Freddy, let us be going. The sooner we have located Lady Redmond, the sooner we can return to Paris and then I wish you joy of your Miss Redmond!"

Leverton suppressed a smile, being well able to imagine how far his friend's patience had been tried. Aloud he said to Eleanor, "Even if Lady Redmond has called up Beauvais, I do not think it very likely he will harm her. But, given what Jason learned last night, I must say that this is not the best time for her to have chosen to visit. And the sooner we have her out of there, the better. Besides, I've still some unfinished business with the count. Eleanor, I'll arrange for you to wait in my private parlor."

She nodded and the two men headed for the door of the inn, Leverton looking about for the innkeeper. Behind them, Eleanor smiled grimly to herself.

So it was that a short time later one of the servants announced to Beauvais that he had more visitors. Since the fellow neglected to mention that they were British, Beauvais was taken completely by surprise to see Frederick Leverton and John Witton standing in the doorway of the parlor. His first impulse was to bolt, but the rapid appearance of a pistol in Freddy's right hand stopped him. Beauvais swallowed hard and said "Messieurs, why are you here?"

Grimly Leverton said, "We understand that Lady Redmond has come to call, but we did not see her coach outside. Is she still here?"

Beauvais spread his hands as he replied, "But, messieurs, if a lady comes to call upon me, am I to tell?"

Witton took a step toward the count but Freddy restrained him. "Hold, John. There are other things we want to know about. Such as Miss Redmond's letters."

"Ah, yes, Miss Redmond. And you are here, no doubt, to defend her nonexistent honor?" Beauvais sneered.

This time Witton watched as Leverton seized Beauvais by the collar and said, "We are. We also want the rest of the letters she wrote. It would be a pity to have to shoot you, Beauvais, before you give them to us."

"There are no more letters," Beauvais said boldly.

"No? What a pity. Then I shall have to shoot you straightaway," Freddy replied with a grim smile.

This was more than Beauvais could bear, and trembling slightly, he said, "No, wait. I shall go get the letters. Of course you shall have them. I have no further use for the things and you, Monsieur Leverton, will no doubt find them most entertaining. I shall fetch them and be right back. If you will please to let go of me?"

Still smiling grimly, Freddy said, "No, I think I shall go with you. I should not want you to think we do not trust you, but . . ."

"But you do not," Beauvais concluded bitterly. "Very well, this way."

Leverton did not release the count as they moved toward the doorway of the parlor and Beauvais said to him, "It is absurd of me, no doubt, but I cannot see why you should care what becomes of Mademoiselle Redmond."

"I care," Leverton said with great deliberation, "because the lady is soon going to become my wife."

These words were spoken as the men stepped out into the hallway, their backs toward the foyer, where a footman stood with the door open to admit a young woman. And Freddy had not troubled to keep his voice low as he added, "Should I discover that you have in any way distressed my future wife, I shall take great pleasure in returning to call you to account for it."

It was at that point that the three men were startled to hear Miss Redmond's voice say coolly, "Indeed? Perhaps she will wish to call him to account herself."

And they turned to see Eleanor standing in the foyer, a pistol in her hand pointing straight at the Comte de Beauvais. "Well, Jean-Pierre? Am I to have my letters back, or not?" she said.

23

"Miss Redmond!" Witton and Beauvais said simultaneously.

"Eleanor, what the devil are you doing here?" Leverton demanded, taking long strides toward her. "And where did you get that gun?"

At once Eleanor lowered the pistol. With a rather shaky laugh she said, "Colonel Milford gave it to Lydia. In Brussels. Just before the battle. In case anything should go wrong. She brought it to Paris and I-I borrowed it when we came north."

"You were supposed to wait at the inn," Witton said in measured tones.

"I was anxious to see my mother," Eleanor replied in the same rather husky voice.

"Well, she does not seem to be here," Leverton retorted curtly.

"Indeed?" a frosty voice echoed from the other end of the hallway. "And how did you arrive at that conclusion?"

Startled, everyone turned to see Lady Redmond walking resolutely toward them.

"But—" Leverton began.

"My maid was taken ill and driven 'round to the back, where she has now fully recovered," her ladyship explained curtly. "But what are all of you doing here?"

"Mama, he still has letters I have written and I must retrieve them," Eleanor said with quiet dignity.

"Lady Redmond, if you will take your daughter back to Paris, at once, I shall undertake to get the letters and her jewelry," Freddy said quickly.

Beauvais, meanwhile, tried to take advantage of the confusion to slip away, but Lady Redmond stopped him. "Letters? Jewelry? Monsieur," she said to Beauvais in a voice that turned all eyes upon him, "I expect them to be returned at once."

"At what price, Lady Redmond?" Beauvais asked slyly. "Your daughter was willing to pay five hundred pounds. A pity I had to leave Brussels before she could raise that sum."

Lady Redmond did not take her eyes off the count as she spoke to Freddy. "Sir," she said, "you will please accompany the Comte de Beauvais and retrieve everything in his possession that belongs to my daughter. Monsieur, I intend to pay you nothing. Instead, if you refuse, I shall be forced to use the pistol *I* have brought."

"Pistols! Everyone has pistols," the count said in exasperation. "And if you shoot me, how will you get your letters then?" Beauvais demanded impudently.

Again Lady Redmond raised her eyebrows. "Oh, I shall not shoot to kill," she said. "I shall merely wound you. First in one arm, then in one leg, and then I shall begin upon the other side."

Frederick Leverton's shoulders could be seen to quiver with suppressed laughter at the look of outrage on the count's face. As Lady Redmond removed the pistol from her reticule, however, the color drained from Beauvais' face and he said hastily to Freddy, "Monsieur, this way."

"And I pray you hurry," Lady Redmond said, pointing the pistol directly at him. "I am impatient to go on to Paris."

"Quickly, Monsieur Leverton, I do not trust these English ladies, they are all mad," Beauvais said to Freddy.

Together they went down the hallway and Lady Redmond lowered her pistol as she turned to John Witton. "I do not wish to appear ungrateful, sir, but may I ask how you come to be here with my daughter? It appears most irregular to me."

"I did not wish to come with Miss Redmond," Witton explained quietly. "But she insisted upon coming and I could not let her come alone."

"Indeed?" Lady Redmond said frostily. "And why did Mrs. Milford neither stop her nor accompany Nora herself? Or Colonel Milford? Who were you to do so?"

"I am a friend of Colonel and Mrs. Milford as well as Freddy Leverton," Witton explained. "Colonel Milford and Mr. Leverton were already here, at the request of the Duke of Wellington, to investigate some disturbing rumors. Therefore, they could not accompany your daughter. Or stop her. As for Mrs. Milford," Witton paused, and his voice grew a trifle bitter as he said, "she was laid down on her bed with a twisted ankle, dosed with laudanum by doctor's orders, and never had a chance to know what was afoot."

Lady Redmond regarded her daughter with raised eyebrows as she said, "Is this true, Nora?"

Eleanor avoided her mother's eyes as she

replied, defensively, "I did not wish to worry Mrs. Milford when she was feeling so poorly. And I could not convince Mr. Witton to let me come alone."

"I should think not!" Lady Redmond said with feeling. Turning to him, she said, "It seems I must thank you, sir."

Witton merely bowed and said quietly, "I would feel better if we could leave here as quickly as possible, Lady Redmond, after Freddy returns with your daughter's letters and jewelry. Mrs. Milford will be concerned, by now, and in any event, according to Freddy, at some point, very soon, certain rather unsavory men may be arriving to visit the count."

But it was as though Lady Redmond had not heard Witton. Instead, she asked her daughter in the frostiest of voices, "What I should like to know, Nora, is why you were so determined to come here?"

Eleanor spoke in a rather tiny voice as she replied, "Amanda wrote that she thought you meant to come here on your way to Paris and confront Beauvais, and I wanted to come stop you. He is a dangerous man."

Lady Redmond raised her eyebrows in disbelief.

With great sangfroid Witton said, "One must suppose Miss Redmond's courage does her credit."

"My daughter's actions may do credit to her courage," Lady Redmond replied sarcastically, "but I cannot say that they do credit to either her intelligence or her sense of propriety."

"Some things are more important than propriety," Eleanor retorted hotly.

Again Lady Redmond raised her eyebrows in

disbelief. "And what did you imagine you could do for me if I was in danger?" she asked frostily.

Eleanor's shoulders slumped as she replied, "I-I don't know."

With a sigh of exasperation Lady Redmond said to John Witton, "What am I going to do with my daughter?"

Gravely he replied, "I advise you to marry her off to Frederick Leverton, as soon as possible. He is the gentleman who went with the count, just now."

"I know who Mr. Leverton is," Lady Redmond replied in her most daunting voice. "I have made it my business to know who all the eligible bachelors are among the *ton*. But may I remind you that I should first have to consult with Lord Redmond before we could speak of marriage? Even if Mr. Leverton does wish to wed my daughter. And my daughter wishes to marry him."

"I do," Eleanor said immediately.

"But he doesn't even have a title," Lady Redmond protested. "To be sure his inheritance is quite respectable, but—"

In exasperation Eleanor cut her mother short. "Do you really think I care?" she demanded.

Lady Redmond regarded her daughter sternly. "One ought always to choose with one's head as well as with one's heart."

Beside them Witton coughed. Once he had their attention, he said quietly, "Lady Redmond, do you truly relish trying to keep a rein on your daughter for the next year or two until her choice settles on someone *you* approve? If it ever does? Having become well-acquainted with her these past weeks, I cannot say it is a task *I* would look forward to. My dear lady I strongly suggest you allow your daughter to marry Leverton!"

While he was speaking, Leverton had returned to the hallway, where the others were waiting, a now-silent Beauvais in tow. His eyes were once more dancing as he said, "Indeed, Lady Redmond. I quite agree with Witton. Given your daughter's penchant for impetuous action, I should not like to wager what she might do if you thwart her." Then he turned to Eleanor and held out a packet of letters as he said, "See if that is the last of the lot. He claims that it is, but I would not trust Beauvais not to hold some back."

"They are all here," she replied after a few moments.

"Are you certain?" Lady Redmond demanded.

"Yes."

"Good, then we may burn these others," Freddy said, showing them another batch of letters he held.

"No," Lady Redmond said, holding out her hand imperiously. "Give them to me and I shall see that they are returned to their rightful owners. Unread. Otherwise Beauvais may stoop so low as to claim he still holds them."

Leverton handed over the letters with a smile and a flourish, saying, "I bow to your superior judgment, Lady Redmond."

She smiled thinly in return, then said, "And did you find my daughter's jewelry?"

"He claims he was obliged to pawn them," Leverton said dryly.

Lady Redmond sighed. "Ah, well, it does not signify. Her father will simply buy her more."

Leverton moved to Eleanor's side, took her hand in his, and ignoring Lady Redmond's gasp of outrage, said with a reassuring smile for Eleanor, "On the contrary, it is I who shall buy her more,

Lady Redmond. I collect you still do not believe it, but I intend to marry your daughter."

"Even though I've a penchant for impetuous action?" Eleanor asked innocently.

"Even so. Though I do not promise not to beat you if you provoke me too far," Freddy replied, his words belied by the warmth with which he smiled at her.

"And you said that *I* behaved improperly," Beauvais protested to everyone indignantly.

"This is most improper," Lady Redmond agreed with some asperity. "But nothing compared to your behavior, monsieur. It is, however, all of a piece with everything else. And I daresay Lord Redmond will have to give his permission. *If* the both of you and I ever get back safely to Paris and then to London. As I recall, some of you appear to believe that there is a degree of danger in this vicinity."

Courteously Witton said, "Lady Redmond, you are welcome to accompany us back to Paris. But if you preferred, you could go straight to the coast from here and board a ship to England."

"No I could not," she retorted with the same asperity as before. "I have with me my personal maid, Penelope. And if you think that creature is capable of returning to sea this quickly, you much mistake the matter. Besides," she said after a brief pause, "I have not visited Paris since before the war. Since I was a child, in fact. I've no intention of rushing away from it now. Nor," she added, forestalling her daughter, "do I have any intention of letting you rush off to London with Mr. Leverton, Nora. We shall all return to Paris and from there he may write your father a very civil letter asking for your hand in marriage and I shall send one along advising him to give his consent. Now come along, everyone, I don't mean to wait here all day. Good bye, Beauvais.''

"Good day," the Frenchman replied emphatically. He watched grimly as Lady Redmond swept out of the château.

The others followed as quickly as they could. Lady Redmond stepped into her carriage while Witton mounted his horse. Freddy handed Eleanor into the other carriage and then started to climb in himself.

"Mr. Leverton!" Lady Redmond said in shocked accents. "You cannot ride unchaperoned with my daughter. Nora, come here. You shall ride with me."

"You forget, Lady Redmond," he replied amiably, "that John has already ridden alone with your daughter in coming here. And while you might prefer him as a son-in-law, I assure you that it would not suit."

Then, ignoring her ladyship's gasp of outrage, Leverton ordered the driver to go. Since he took the precaution of promising the fellow a handsome tip if he did so, they pulled away at top speed and Lady Redmond had no choice but to follow in her own coach at a more decorous speed. And, with another laugh, Witton took charge of Freddy's horse and rode back to the inn to collect his baggage for him.

Meanwhile, inside the first carriage, Frederick Leverton was regarding Eleanor Redmond intently. For some odd reason she kept evading his eyes and finally he said, sternly, "We've some unfinished business, you know."

Eleanor swallowed and nodded, still avoiding his eyes. "Are you very angry with me?" she asked in a small voice.

Leverton imprisoned both her wrists with one hand and in a swift motion pulled her across his lap as he said grimly, "I promised you a spanking if you didn't do as you were told, and I am strongly tempted to give it to you here and now!"

As answer, Eleanor shut her eyes and buried her head against his chest, crushing the brim of her bonnet in the process. "You are furious with me, aren't you?" she asked in the same small voice as before.

"Only because for some unfathomable reason I happen to be in love with you and care for your safety," Leverton retorted, a smile beginning to soften the corners of his mouth. Gently he undid the ribbons under her chin and removed her bonnet. A moment later his chin came to rest on the top of her head and he said with a chuckle, "I suppose I ought to ask if you are angry with me for taking so high-handed a tone with your mother."

She shook her head shyly. "No, but Mama is furious," she replied with something of a giggle.

Gently Leverton tilted up Eleanor's chin so that he could see her face as he said, with un-accustomed seriousness, "You do still wish to marry me, don't you?"

"More than anything in the world," Eleanor replied earnestly.

The customary twinkle again appeared in Leverton's eyes as he said, "Even though I am such a high-handed fellow and threaten to beat you? And am completely lacking in any sense of what is proper?"

As an answer, Eleanor kissed Freddy and his arms tightened around her so that she could scarcely breathe. When he finally let her go, Eleanor told him, "Oh, Freddy, I do love you!"

"That," he said with a shaky laugh, "is fortunate, since our coachman appears to have forgotten to stop at the inn and may not let us out of here until we reach Paris. I'm afraid, my dear, that if it were not already true, you would soon be completely compromised."

Snuggling close against his shoulder, Eleanor replied, "So long as it is with you, I don't care a fig. Particularly not when you have already offered to marry me. I only want to be with you."

"And so you shall be," he promised, "for the rest of our lives."

With a contented sigh, Eleanor kissed him again.

About the Author

April Lynn Kihlstrom was born in Buffalo, New York, and graduated from Cornell University with an M.S. in Operations Research. She, her husband, and their two children enjoy traveling and have lived in Paris, Honolulu, Georgia, and New Jersey. When not writing, April Lynn Kihlstrom enjoys needlework and devotes her time to handicapped children.

COMING IN JULY 1988

Eileen Jackson
A Servant of Quality

Mary Jo Putney
The Would-Be Widow

Anita Mills
The Duke's Double

The New Super Regency
Edith Layton
The Game of Love

SIGNET REGENCY ROMANCE

COMING IN JULY!

A new realm of romance and passion—
in Signet's Super Regency novels . . .

The GAME of LOVE
EDITH LAYTON

author of the award-winning *Love in Disguise*
*A fiery beauty dares to yield to her passion for a
handsome stranger with a shadowy past . . .*

Beautiful Francesca Wyndham was taking a
gamble when she fell in love with Arden Lyons,
a gentleman who was clearly anything but when
it came to winning what he wanted: a hand of
cards, a test of strength, or a lady's favors.
Though Francesca knew nothing about this man
. . . though his past was a dark mystery . . .
she dared to pit her innocence against his ex-
pertise. It was definitely a game where passion
took all. . . .

There's an epidemic with 27 million victims. And no visible symptoms.

It's an epidemic of people who can't read.

Believe it or not, 27 million Americans are functionally illiterate, about one adult in five.

The solution to this problem is you... when you join the fight against illiteracy. So call the Coalition for Literacy at toll-free **1-800-228-8813** and volunteer.

Volunteer Against Illiteracy. The only degree you need is a degree of caring.